DEMON Q

NEW VAMPIRE DISORDER, BOOK 8

MARIE JOHNSTON

LE PUBLISHING

Xan is used to going it alone. After all, there's no one else to trust when you're a demon in the underworld. But when the only two people she's ever cared about are snatched and held to ensure her good behavior, she'll do anything—or anyone —to get them back. So when she's ordered to spy on a hideous, arrogant energy demon, she doesn't blink...until Quution starts to look less like the enemy and more like salvation.

Quution never cared how ugly his disguise was until *she* started showing up, asking innocuous questions and distracting him with her curves. Now he wishes the beauty knew he wasn't such a beast. But he didn't rise to the ruling circle of the underworld on might alone, and he won't let Xan ferret out his secrets. Because Quution's hiding one that'll rock the underworld and change the fate of demons forever...if no one stops him first.

The chemistry between them is more than a case of opposites attract. But time's running out for Xan, and as she gets closer to unraveling Quution's plans, both will be forced to choose between the destruction of the realms or saying goodbye forever.

CHAPTER 1

"*S*o whaddya say, Electrocution?" Xan taunted. The demon glaring at her hated when she messed up his name. So she made sure to do it on a daily basis.

Which also meant she'd been going out of her way to cross paths with him daily. Not an easy task in the underworld with its maze of passages, catacombs, and caverns.

It was like the damn demon had a homing beacon on him that led her straight to him. He was hideous and arrogant, yet she always had a hard time leaving the chamber she found him in.

"It's Quution," he gritted for the one thousandth two hundred and eighty-second time. She'd been counting.

She made sure her voice dripped with innocence. "Oh, is that how it's pronounced?"

As she spun away to study the books lining this particular hole in the wall she'd found him in, a low growl bounced off the walls. The corner of her mouth kicked up.

Score. She'd gotten to him.

She listed random titles off the top of her head, hoping at least one was in his collection. "*A Tale of Two Cities*? *Treasure*

Island? *Anne of Green Gables*? Who reads this shit?" Jealousy snaked through her. He probably did. She couldn't read human languages. She couldn't read her *own* language. There was a reason most demons used pictographs. Their claws got in the way of holding a writing utensil.

She glanced down at her own nails. Sharpened to pert points, they weren't much longer than a human's and fit her humanoid form.

Only humans weren't purple like she was.

"I don't know, Nebula. Perhaps people who like to broaden their thinking beyond kill, eat, fuck."

She briefly shut her eyes. Quution saying "fuck" did naughty things to her insides. Why? Why him of all demons? He lurched more than walked. And he wore clothing like a heathen. A huge tent-like trench coat with raggedy canvas pants and platform boots.

Who was the monster humans used to fear? Xan hadn't been to the movies in decades, preferring documentaries. What was his name? Frankenstein?

Yeah. Quution shared a wardrobe with Frankenstein. And he probably had Mary Shelley on his shelves.

Xan kicked her shoulders back. There. She was just as smart as him. "Why do you call me by that name? *Nebula*. I'm not an interstellar cloud of dust." Suck it, demon. She could Google shit, too, thanks to voice search. She craned her head around to peer at him.

Quution cast a droll look her way from where he sat hunched over a carved wooden desk. How the hell had he squirreled that down here? She suspected he'd brought all the items here from the human realm only to show off his staggering power, an ability that had painted a target on his smelly jacket.

Actually, his coat smelled like a fresh field she'd once run through when she'd possessed a human child in the 1700s. It hadn't been a flight of pleasure, and that was perhaps the reason why the scent clung to her memory. She hadn't been fast enough to carry the child away from danger.

She'd never possessed a child again. Her current human host was a six-foot-four gym bro, but she hadn't had to use him often. Not since Quution had stormed onto the Circle of Thirteen and taken over.

He made quite the target.

"Nebula is an assassin in the Marvel universe," he said.

She tensed briefly. Why an assassin? "I thought humans only thought they had one universe. Or did you mean galaxy?" Had she bested Quution on a topic?

He stared at her like he couldn't believe she'd even asked. "Perhaps the next time you hit the human realm, you should go to a movie theater. They are quite the hoot." He tipped his head back down to read the tome in front of him.

"Why an assassin?" she blurted. All demons killed. Being sneaky about it was more of a sign of weakness down here, unlike with humans, who regarded assassins as skilled hunters. And she wasn't an assassin, just…stealthy.

Quution sighed and lifted his lilac gaze off the page. His sunset-orange horns stuck out of his shaggy mahogany hair. Half the time, they pointed in different directions. How humiliating.

Then why couldn't she quit staring at them, wondering if he had touch receptors in them? If she stroked them—

No pleasure. She wasn't interested in how good anything felt for Quution. Weakness was her strength, fear specifically. An easy target for a sort-of empath like her. Others of her kind could detect a target's weaknesses through other emotions, but not her.

"Because you resemble her and she's an assassin in the movies." He went back to reading.

It was like Quution was sensing *her* weakness. She hated

being dismissed as insignificant. At six feet tall, she was still shorter than many demons. And she was only a half-breed, not full and not terrifying to look at like a full-blood. Like Quution.

Only she wasn't terrified by him. She was mesmerized. Bizarrely fascinated.

His fangs stuck out so far they pushed his lower lip in. There was nothing attractive about him.

Well, those eyes, but no one would blame a purple girl for liking another shade of purple.

Nebula from the Marvel universe. She'd have to look that up, see herself from Quution's eyes. Perhaps she would pop into her host just to check. It was another way to delay her report to another member of the Circle. Spaeth. She despised the male, but he currently had her by the short hairs—or would have, if she'd had any hair.

XAN'S BRIMSTONE scent filled the room. The sulfur smell was part of him, part of his surroundings, but when Xan entered a room, her brimstone scent was…different. Enticingly different. There was a hint of lavender underneath. A purple flower to match her purple skin, though her hue was much darker.

Her eyes were nearly a solid black, but when he looked close enough—not that he ever did—they were actually a rich eggplant. Swirls of lighter purple lined her skin and were the only reason he hadn't called her Mystique. Both characters were pigmented and deadly, but Xan's eyes held a hint of vulnerability. It was why Nebula had popped into his head.

That was ridiculous. Xan's specialty was targeting weak points in a person, whether it was their darkest fears or personal demons or a coveted treasure.

Why she hounded him down here, he couldn't guess, but she was up to something.

For years, all he'd had were himself and his smarts. Xan had a plan and he was involved and he probably wouldn't like it.

If he were more ambitious, he'd figure out what she was up to, but part of him didn't want to know that she wasn't bugging him because she had a raging crush. Disappointment was too much of a constant companion. As much as loneliness was.

He was so busy searching the records of his kind that she was sometimes the only being he talked to all day. All of his vampire—dare he say friends?—were happily mated and the underworld was fairly stable.

It wouldn't last forever. There were too many loopholes in their governing system, if he could call it that. Part of the reason he was so isolated was to avoid dominance challenges for his position. One, he didn't like killing others. Two, it was a time suck. Three, no one could best him anyway.

But the other Circle members were different. Even demons could have an off day and lose a fight, including those who'd won their spot on the Circle. Through meticulous intervention, he'd seeded part of the Circle with half-breeds, but they wouldn't stay there for long if he didn't find a way to prevent another upheaval from happening. And he'd bet his left toenails that the full-bloods were planning one. They couldn't get past being ruled by half-breeds, and they certainly resented the necessity of cavorting with vampires to access the human realm. How full-bloods could be cunning and manipulative, yet dumb as a stone left him shaking his head.

Demons wanted more access to what they all called the human realm, despite the other creatures that lived there. It was humans that made creatures like him stick to the shadows. Their sheer numbers made them impossible to conquer or enslave, though that didn't stop demons from trying. His kind wasn't known for following the rules in any realm.

Xan sauntered closer. It was getting harder and harder to keep his eyes above her collar. She had the ripest breasts. His fangs throbbed every time they were visible in his peripheral vision. Even his prosthetic fangs ached.

He should shove her away instead of watching her bare ass slide across the top of the desk. Her scent bloomed in his nose until his blood rushed south.

The last thing he needed around the demoness was an erection. She'd bite it off and tease him with it.

He might let her.

Only she'd find that he wasn't all that he seemed and he couldn't let that happen. She couldn't get under his clothing. He didn't know who she was spying for, but his half-breed lineage had to stay secret. Full-bloods didn't exactly trust him, but sometimes they couldn't help themselves and treated him like "one of them." To them, any full-blood was better than a half-breed.

Sweet brimstone, he couldn't wait until he didn't have to wear this gaudy outfit anymore. Only he wasn't sure he could wander around nude. He'd been covered up in this realm since he'd first interacted with someone other than his mother. Wearing clothing would be suspicious, especially after what his sire had done, but Quution's attire served another purpose.

Not many beings could carry items between realms, but he was an energy demon. Every being had energy, electrical currents running through them. Even inanimate objects possessed potential energy, which meant he could manipulate nearly everything. Displaying all his human-realm possessions was a show of his power, and a reminder of the bounty he could share with his full-blood "allies"—if he chose to. That Xan meddled with him when she thought he was a full-blood was either a show of her own power or... He wasn't sure what. He couldn't figure her out.

"What do all the vamps call you?" Her purr was too close to his ear. "Q?"

He jerked his head up. She was leaning over, her gaze dropping to the tome he was reading and back up to his eyes.

"Yes. Sometimes." His brother especially. He fought the urge to tell her more. Was that one of her powers? Or just the allure of a beautiful demon?

Funny, he'd thought that with all his studies, he'd fall for a human. A vampire at the very least. Why a demon?

On the desk, she was positioned higher than him, her breasts dangerously at eye level. He forced his gaze to stay up.

She cocked her head and arched a black brow. "Whatcha reading, Q?" Her gaze brushed the page, but a small frown marred her lush lips.

He studied her closely. Not a hardship, but he had to know if she could understand what was on the page.

She couldn't. Her expression remained blank, though, with a hint of frustration. Since she'd rattled off titles absent from his library, he guessed she couldn't read many languages, if any at all. Not many demons could. *Why educate a population you want to control?* had been the former Circle's attitude.

He wouldn't be able to read, either, except that having been imprisoned with his mother for much of his early life, he'd learned to pass the time. "I'm catching up on Albrecht Dürer's theories for the geometrical construction of complex polyhedra." Watching her reaction, he waited for her to call bullshit.

"Why would you read that?" She brushed a long finger over the page. Was that reverence in her eyes?

Ah. She wanted to know how to read.

He regretted his words before he said them, but they were necessary. "To keep my mind sharp. You should try it sometime."

She stiffened and slid off the table. "My mind is as sharp as my claws, demon."

His gaze touched on where her round, muscular ass had been. What he wouldn't give for just one chance to ogle her properly. But he couldn't bring himself to do it.

Two main reasons. He'd seen firsthand what unwanted male attention did to a female. And he'd also seen the atrocious fallout of a male trying to pull off full-blooded status and what it had done to him and his mate—and their young.

Xan wasn't staying away from him no matter how much he tried to evade her, so he'd have to stoop to insults. Because if she was even a little bit receptive to his lack of charm, he might be willing to throw his life's plans away.

CHAPTER 2

*X*an stormed into her personal chamber. That horrid, arrogant demon.

She'd meant only to determine what tome he was reading and he'd called her stupid. No one but her own mama had insulted her as much.

"Other demons call us fear demons, but in your case, it's true. That's all your meager senses can read. I don't know why I should claim such a stunning disappointment."

She tried to shake off Mama's criticisms, but damn. Quution's dismissive attitude toward her abilities had brought them all rushing back. Though her kind were called fear demons, it was because of the emotion they inspired in their prey. They actually sensed the full spectrum of emotion. All the better to identify a weak point—and then brutally exploit it. Mama had been able to twist even the smallest, most benign thoughts and emotions into stark terror. But thanks to her weak half-breed powers, Xan could only ferret out a being's weaknesses via fear, terror, or worry —emotions even a newborn fear demon could read.

Xan's upper lip curled to reveal a fang. The tiny nubs

wouldn't strike fear in any creature in the underworld, but it didn't mean she hadn't ripped tracheas out with them. Well, only a few. Okay, one, but that particular demon hadn't feared anything.

She might've been Mama's biggest disappointment, but Mama had taught her how to fight.

Storming to her cavern, she thought of all the ways she'd love to wipe the smugness off Quution's face. Grab his horns and swing her heels into his gut. Cover his clothes in centaur drool and light him on fire. Yank his fangs out with toothpicks.

Grab his face and lay a big, wet kiss on those full lips.

She ran a hand over her bare scalp. Her tumultuous thoughts couldn't be trusted. She needed to sneak into the human realm and pump some iron.

After wiggling her fingers over the entrance to set her wards, she went to the far corner and tapped on a section of the wall that resembled granite. It slid open to reveal a chamber that had nothing but dust and enough air to keep her breathing. She stepped inside and shut the panel behind her. Dots of light snuck in through the uneven edges, enough to prevent suffocation.

She was surprised more demons weren't killed upon their return from Earth. To get topside in the first place, a demon's body left the realm and squatted in a human. That was all fine and dandy, except when they returned to the underworld, their body popped back into existence in the exact spot they'd left from. Unless that spot was well protected, the moment they returned the demon was as vulnerable as a candy beetle to anyone lying in wait. But demons weren't known for their patience, and waiting for their prey to return to the realm—when it wasn't known where exactly they'd appear—was boring.

She'd tried it a few times.

When she was home, the wards to her chamber alerted her if a demon tried to enter, but if she was gone when it happened, by the time she returned and opened her eyes, she could be shanked already. Or worse. But if they couldn't find her, they couldn't get the jump on her. The few years spent carving out the concealed closet had been worth it.

Smart demons hid themselves.

And she hadn't known then that she'd be coerced into fighting for a position on the Circle. As if she'd ever wanted to herd feral, rabid cats. Now she watched her back more than she'd ever had in her life. No thanks. Isolation was how she preferred things. Except for her sister.

Xera was the exception to everything.

Settling on the floor, she regulated her breathing and concentrated. Her host was resistant, but never enough to block her. He'd willingly recited the incantation to allow her possession. No take backs.

Opening Marcus's eyes, she gasped. A barbell with three massive weights on each side was primed above her head. She flinched and shoved upward. A guy who lived in Marcus's building was spotting her, caught the bar and racked it.

"Marcus?" The man—what did Marcus call him?—*Digger* was coming around to peer at her. But while she was in control, Marcus's eyes would be ink black.

She groaned at the stiffness in her bent arms. Why'd Marcus insist on killing himself in the gym? She gazed down at the chicken legs that were now hers to command. Would it hurt him to do some calf raises?

As a humanoid demon who lacked spikes, scales, or thorns, she relied on balance and agility to survive. The first time she'd controlled Marcus, she'd nearly tipped face-first into a pyramid of dumbbells. The guy was top-heavy, his biceps busting out of his sleeves. His chest was as round as a barrel and his abs rippled with an eight-pack. But then his thighs started the extreme taper that ended at his size fourteens.

"I'm fine." Marcus's rumble was always startling to hear at first instead of her own voice. "I have a headache. Gotta go."

She left the weight area, ignored the bare asses in the locker room, and snagged Marcus's keys. Before she left the gym to find his car, she sat on a bench and thumbed his phone on. Using voice commands, she looked up Nebula of the Marvel universe.

She frowned at the picture that came up of a petite, somewhat blue female with unusual markings and black eyes. "I look nothing like her."

A guy at his locker with a towel slung over his waist turned around, his brow raised.

Xan shot him a glare. Easy to do. Perma-glare was Marcus's default expression. But she couldn't hold it or the guy would look too close at her eyes.

His gaze dropped to the phone. "You're both bald, but she's hot and you're not." He turned back to getting dressed, dropping his towel in the process.

Nice ass.

Argh. Why'd she have to find humanoid forms attractive? Tentacles didn't do it for her and that was why she'd broken it off with Cremor. Then there was the male who had been supremely offended when she wouldn't let him use either one of his horns as a sex toy. If her vagina hadn't been purple before, it would've been afterward. What had his name been? And then there had been Zor. Scales just shouldn't cover some body parts. When they'd parted, she'd told him there was some demoness out there with an armored vag for him.

She scrolled through more pictures. That human thought this creature was hot? What did Quution think?

She bared her teeth, but Marcus didn't have fangs.

Enough of this. She fisted his keys. She might not read, but over the centuries, she'd adapted. The current period was her favorite, and walking around as a big man in this realm meant she wasn't bothered by anyone. Except for that one time someone had called the cops on her host for breaking into his own car when she'd locked the keys inside.

The drive to Marcus's apartment was short. She kicked his tennies off and flopped on the couch. Air conditioning with no smell of rot.

A tingle vibrated over her being.

Fuck. Someone was at her wards.

Ugh, what if it was Spaeth? She'd better get back and answer him.

Time for the dreaded report to her boss. *Marcus, fuel up. The body is yours now.*

~

QUUTION TAPPED his finger against the tabletop. The sizzle of bacon from behind the counter teased his nose.

"Sure you don't want some?" Stryke asked. His sunglasses were perched on the hat he wore to hide his own horns.

Quution shifted in the booth. He and Stryke were meeting at a diner that served breakfast twenty-four/seven, and Zoey had come along. His brother had ordered the bacon. So had every other patron in the place.

"No, thank you." *Fuck, yes.*

He couldn't eat that type of food in the underworld, and his host shouldn't be eating it in any realm.

Two plates were slid in front of them. Stryke's was loaded with sausage and bacon that he and Zoey would share. Quution's had an egg white omelet with spinach. It looked unappetizing. The bacon smell sank into Quution's pores until he thought he'd gnaw off his arm, but he only

13

smiled politely as Stryke slid his plate in between him and Zoey.

Quution tracked Stryke as he lifted each piece to his lips, then followed his hand back down. Yes, that slice looked extra fatty. Quution's mouth watered, and if he wasn't careful, drool would run down his host's chin. And it would be no different than when he tried to eat in his chamber.

Stryke tossed a piece in front him. "Just eat it. You look like you're going to make love to my plate."

Yes, well, Quution wouldn't know where to start, would he? He speared the meat with his fork and managed not to moan when he bit off a chunk.

"You're among family, Q," Zoey said, her gaze still on her iPad while he caught up his brother. "You can eat it all in one bite and we won't judge."

Family. He'd reconnected with his brother, the murder attempt from the first time they'd met forgiven, and were now working together. To the rest of the underworld, Stryke was just Quution's half-breed flunky, a common arrangement for full-bloods on the Circle, but they were more like partners.

"Thank you for the offer." Quution finished his delicacy and wiped his fingers on a napkin. "But this host has atrocious cholesterol levels. His heart grunts each time it beats."

His brother eyed him. They looked so similar, but no one would know it if they stood side by side while Quution was in disguise. Quution's eyes were a lighter purple, his hair a darker brown. His horns resembled a fading sunset. They were similar in height and build, but with his platform shoes, Quution was taller, even though he purposely walked lopsided and had the backache to prove it.

"What?" Quution asked when Stryke didn't look away.

"You've gotten more…proper."

Quution dropped his voice. "I'm a demon." He was in a host. He had to blend.

"Could've fooled me." Stryke went back to his food. He shoved a morsel in his mouth and muttered, "But that atrocious getup you wear in the underworld helps."

Yes, it did. But "more proper"? So what if he might act more formal lately. The vampires kept looking to him for answers to existential questions. Just the other night, Melody had come to him with worries about being Creed's one and only. *What if he has a true mate?*

Creed had Melody for a mate. Why would fate give him another? Fate was logical. Beings were cruel.

Take his father, and how he'd pretended to be a full-blood and fooled the underworld. Until Stryke was born, threatening their sire's secret.

Family didn't mean the same thing to Quution. The way Zoey used the word indicated implicit trust, but while Quution trusted Stryke, he was in no hurry to strip down and strut around in his true form in front of anyone. He couldn't even be in this realm as himself the way Stryke could. The furthest he'd ever gotten was projecting an image of himself, and that had drained his energy nearly dry.

"I think one of the full-bloods is on to me," Quution said.

Stryke abandoned his food. How could he not finish each crumble of greasy meat? Had the accessibility of food that didn't thrive in the cesspools of the underworld ruined Stryke? Quution's stomach threatened to rumble. Zoey had better finish it or he would lick the plate, manners be damned.

"Is someone giving you trouble?" Stryke's eyes flashed.

"Not trouble. Xan is snooping."

Stryke frowned. "She's the purple one, right?"

"Indeed." Eggplant. The swirls of lighter shades streaking through her were never in the same exact spot. And they tended to shift with her moods. "I have not yet determined what she's after." *But I will*.

"Isn't she a fear demon?" Stryke asked.

"That's what they call her kind, yes." He'd heard rumors they were more like empaths, but regardless, the underworld gave purple demons like her a wide berth. "I keep a tight lid on my feelings when she's around. Yet she keeps coming around."

"Maybe she's into you?" Zoey wasn't teasing. It was a valid conclusion to rule out. Quution had considered the fact for much longer than he cared to admit.

"She has a type. It's not me." His chest constricted at the words. No, Xan's last few partners had resembled his brother more than Quution's current appearance.

Not that he'd noticed.

Stryke nodded, as if it was easy to accept amour couldn't be the reason. "Do you think they suspect you plan to form a ward between our realms?"

"Ward" was a weak word. It was to be an ironclad binding that would forever prevent total full-blood rule of the human realm. Full-bloods would no longer be able to barter and negotiate with human hosts, obliterating any hopes of taking over this realm.

And when it was all said and done and the dust of the underworld had settled, Quution would be up here, with his brother, living with people who weren't trying to kill him and who he could actually converse with.

No, his plan would not be popular. Both realms would be protected. Humans would no longer be able to call demons to their bidding—usually getting tricked in the process. And demons would only have one realm to terrorize.

Stryke yanked him out of his own mind. "What are you going to do about Xan?"

Quution wondered that every day. "She's one of the

Circle. There's not much I can do." Just because they had both attained a spot on the Circle didn't mean they treated each other as colleagues or equals. The Circle was full of backstabbing power mongers, even the half-breeds he'd maneuvered into place. Sharing power with twelve other demons just wasn't natural. Demons were always plotting ways to manipulate the power structure, and that usually included killing another member to make room for their buddy, whom they'd also stab in the back for an advantageous outcome at a later date.

So it was a given that Xan was up to something. "But I'll keep an eye on her."

But he wouldn't really *watch* her, or he'd go insane. He longed to trace the swirls of her long, graceful neck—with his tongue. Was her skin as soft as it looked?

He cleared his throat and turned his lust toward the greasy plate. Seriously, was Stryke not going to eat the crumbs?

Stryke ducked his head to catch Quution's eye. "Why didn't you just order the bacon?"

Because he was possessing another being. He didn't need to contribute to the plaque in the man's arteries. Quution scowled. "Fill me in while I eat."

He dug into his bland omelet before it got too cold and lost what flavor there was. It was still better than the scavenger bugs roaming the underworld. Food was as close to heaven as a demon could get and even a blah omelet was better than a putrid beetle.

As Quution ate, Stryke filled him in, his voice pitched low. Eavesdroppers would only hear a murmur. "Demon possessions have skyrocketed. Now that the Synod is at full strength, it's like the vampires opposing them and their regulations have launched into a last-ditch effort to take over the realm."

Quution swallowed his mouthful. "That's impossible."

The entire circle would need to be in the realm at once. Finding hosts wasn't easy, and getting thirteen demons to act in unison to recite the incantations that would allow them to take over the earth would be difficult at best.

They'd have to know the work-around, like he did. But even without it, they could disrupt the realm enough to cause problems for the Synod.

Stryke said his fears out loud. "Demetrius is afraid they're running us ragged on purpose."

"We're all out almost every night," Zoey added. "There's no such thing as shifts. I think the full-bloods that have vampire hosts and the lower demons working for them are intentionally spreading us thin."

Quution's hand clenched his fork. In his own form, he would've warped the utensil. That was exactly what the demons were doing. Demetrius and his team were the vampires standing between the underworld and a hostile takeover of the human realm. Absurdly, there were plenty of vampires who despised Demetrius enough to side with demons and aid them. Of course the demons always lied about their true intentions and whether or not the vampires would end up enslaved with the rest or not. It didn't matter. Those that plotted against Demetrius and the Synod only cared that he be destroyed in the process. Any perceived benefits were a bonus. The only species benefitting from a direct, unfiltered portal to the underworld was the demons.

"Are you close, Q?" Stryke barely mouthed the words. The risk was real. Quution was dangerously close to the top of the underworld's most wanted list as it was.

"Yes. But it still requires several more hours of research." He wouldn't get a second chance to carry out his plans. "And I have three more specimens to obtain."

His little work-around required a physical piece of each

Circle member. Gathering the collection had consumed more time than he'd expected. Each time a changeup happened, it was out with the old, in with the new. Like the death of Spawn. His replacement on the Circle was Spaeth, and the radioactive bastard was hard to get to.

"We'll give you as much time as we can," Stryke said.

"But you need to hurry," Zoey added, going back to catching up on the news. Quution took a good look at her. Fatigue weighed her shoulders down, and her usually steely eyes were more like dull lead. She'd be back to no-nonsense Zoey once she left the diner with Stryke, but for the moment her walls were down. She was scared for her people and working tirelessly to save them.

He needed to gather the information and items for the wards. Only, as he went back to picking at his flavorless breakfast, he couldn't claim not to care about what happened to all the beings in the underworld once he sealed them in. One demon in particular stood out in his mind. And he couldn't stop wondering what would happen to her.

CHAPTER 3

*X*an kept a rigid hold on her breathing. By the time she'd returned, Spaeth had left. So she'd had to go in search of him, trying not to think about how much more the extra time would anger him. Spaeth flitted around her now—in one spot on her inhale, in a completely different spot on her exhale. The chamber was warm, and randomly chosen. Spaeth never met her in the same place twice, and never, ever in his personal cave.

As if she didn't know where he lived. And that all these meeting areas were in the vicinity of his home. She'd filed that away for future reference.

He never showed himself for long, appearing and disappearing at will, a moving target, and the main reason he was still alive after the recent Circle upheaval. That, and his nuclear personality. If he stayed in one place for long, the radiation he emitted would bubble the skin right off her.

As it was, blisters formed whenever he appeared. What she wouldn't give for a coat of lead. The bastard. He was crafty and devious and looking at him burned her retinas. Not many beings could withstand a full ogle of Spaeth.

On the bright side, he might've coerced her to work for him, but he didn't think her body was his personal playground. The full-blooded demon was brutal, ambitious, and arrogant—but it was a deserved arrogance. He blackmailed her like a decent demon, utilizing her skills for his benefit. Not once had rape been on the table, or even seduction. Nor did she ever get the feeling that he was plotting to sell her to the highest bidder.

He'd been behind her promotion to one of the Thirteen. It had been part of his demands when he'd first approached her. Since he'd promised to kill her entire family while she watched if she didn't obey, she'd challenged for a seat on the Circle before the day had been done.

I'll burn them to ashes, one layer of skin at a time, while you watch. Claims she didn't doubt he could accomplish.

Only he knew where her sister and niece were—because he'd abducted them. Thus Xan was his faithful servant.

Still, it did a girl good to keep searching for her boss's weaknesses in case she needed to kill him. Correction: in case she got the *opportunity* to kill him.

"What has the demon Q been up to?" Spaeth hissed. Xan almost smiled. Spaeth hated using Quution's name; it was too close to acknowledging that the male had outsmarted him to fill the Circle with half-breeds.

"Research. I haven't determined for what yet."

Spaeth flashed in her face, the wave of radiation breathing agony across her skin.

How did Spaeth mate? On the plus side, he was probably a fast fuck, but his poor partner would shed some cancerous cells once the male finished. She couldn't help studying him. It was what she did with her targets. How did they function? What were their strengths and weaknesses? How could she use that knowledge against them? She'd never relied on her powers alone. There were so many more ways to harvest knowledge on a subject.

Xan excelled in fear and that was it. According to stories she'd been told growing up, she should be able to exploit them to the point of distorting the emotion into her target's biggest nightmare—or fantasy. A fear that was targeted enough, personal enough, could be molded, submerging the victim into a world of their mind's own making, like a hallucination. Half reality, half illusion. Or that's what would happen, if she'd ever done it. According to Mama, she needed to manipulate more emotions than fear to achieve it.

Xan wasn't so sure.

A flash of pain flared on her left. "What's taking you so long?"

"He is secretive and can travel through the realms at will." Damn energy demon. "I hunt him down daily and get closer each time. But he is a high-profile target and I must tread carefully or he will be on to you."

Her subtle comment that Quution would deal not just with her, but also hunt down Spaeth, hadn't been missed. The flash of Spaeth's expression was pure annoyance and it made her heart sing. Another weakness of his. Fear of Quution, and fear of failure.

"Find a way to spend a lot of time around him. Seduce him." Annoyance rang through the chamber.

"He's not indiscriminate."

Spaeth materialized in front of her face. All of her muscles went rigid to refrain from jerking away. "My spies say he's in the human realm now. Why?" He vanished. She blinked against the dryness in her eyes.

"I was also in the realm but didn't have time to find him. I came back for the summons." Hopefully the truthful part of her statement covered the lie.

It'd be nice if his spies could throw her a bone and tell her where Quution went.

Fangs appeared in front of her eyes. "No excuses."

She blinked. Damn, it'd take all day before it felt like she wasn't blinking with sandpaper.

"What's his weakness?"

"I haven't spent enough time with him." She needed more exposure. If the weakness was strong, she could sense it. Fear called to her like a divining rod. All she had to do was be in the same room as the feeling was experienced. It was like the emotion seeped into the rock, tainting it with a resonance that still called to her long after the fact. If a human had to explain it, they'd probably go off on something about pheromones or some real Discovery Channel gibberish, but to her, it just was. The mechanism didn't matter as long as she knew how to use her talent. Well, what little talent she had, anyway. Made living in the underworld super fun. But if her target had tight control over his emotions, her task was even more difficult.

Quution was a deliciously controlled man.

"Then spend enough time with him!" The words came from behind her. Spittle sprayed across her nape, burning in spots where it touched. "I didn't hire you to play hard to get."

He hadn't hired her at all. *As long as you're loyal to me, your sister and her whelp will live.*

She hadn't seen Xera for months. Was she okay? Terrified? Spaeth didn't abuse Xan, but did he abuse her sister? Xan's stomach twisted. Or her wee little niece, Xoda?

Xan hadn't killed her abusive mother with her bare hands only to lose Xera and Xoda to a deranged, power-hungry demon who couldn't do his own dirty work.

How would she stick to Quution like glue? He'd been painfully clear that he didn't see her as a potential mate. He wasn't the type of guy who gathered BFFs for gossip seshes about what the new Circle members were wearing. Except for Quution, they were all nude anyway.

He might keep a tight rein on himself, but she'd been around him enough to know that he prided himself on his intelligence.

Ugh, she hated what she had to do next, but it was sure to appeal to Quution and would guarantee copious amounts of time together.

She lifted her chin. "Fine. Everywhere he turns, he'll see me."

~

SWEET BRIMSTONE, what was she doing here?

Quution froze in his doorway at the sight a purple demon reclining on his bed. He was one of the few demons who had an actual door. Another object he'd smuggled from the human realm, and it hadn't taken nearly as much power as he'd thought.

His gaze swept his chamber. Had she let others in? His need for privacy had him clutching the scrolls he'd borrowed from Demetrius's mate, Calli, to his chest.

The pile of books on the large stone in the corner of his cave was in place. His clothing hung from hooks on the walls, and the faux rock he stored his backup prosthetics in was undisturbed. But he couldn't relax.

A nude Xan lay on his bedding. He'd never experience a peaceful night of sleep again.

As if he had in the first place. After the way he'd grown up, fitful sleeping was all he knew.

"W-what are you doing here?" And how had she found his place? He'd manipulated energy signatures in a mile-wide radius around his chamber to misdirect and confuse would-be visitors. Very few people had been to his home, and each had been invited out of necessity.

"Got a proposal for you, Quution."

Her purr caressed his body. His craving for contact, for another being's touch, nearly drove him to his knees.

He steeled himself. "I'm waiting."

She rose in one lithe move. He gulped and forced his gaze up so high he would've been staring at the ceiling if he hadn't corrected and sought her dark eyes.

So lovely. Mysterious.

Determined.

What was she up to? Would he be smart enough to keep her from whatever her goal was?

She slinked toward him. Even with his gaze firmly on her face, he couldn't miss the swing of her hips. He adjusted the scrolls just to distract himself and keep his blood from pooling in his groin.

"Quution." His name on her lips again. It was like she knew how his energy went haywire when she said it. "You're the only one who can help."

She stopped right under his nose. Lavender laced with brimstone. Humans would wrinkle their noses, but he wanted to lean in, take huge breaths until he infused all his pores with her scent.

He had to get her out of here.

"What do you mean only I can help?" He managed to sound dubious and not horny.

She trailed a finger around the top of one scroll, dangerously close to his skin. Her touch was close enough that his energy reached for her.

A dark brow lifted as she watched him. "I need you, Quution."

He clutched his load tighter and stepped back. He was almost back in the corridor, but he didn't care. This female was dangerous to his sensibilities. She made him want things he'd long given up.

"How could you possibly need me?" She was competent. Capable. Crafty. She'd made it onto the Circle, though he couldn't figure out a reason why. Melody had been the first half-breed to crack the Circle, then Quution had provided opportunities for other half-breeds he'd known, a few demons who wouldn't just use the added power to pad their own pockets. Not that anyone but him had pockets down here. But the half-breeds were stronger than they knew, even if centuries under the rule of full-breeds had disheartened them.

But Xan had come out of nowhere to earn her position by defeating another Circle member and then…done nothing with it.

She gave him a searing look that suggested just how he could be useful. His body warmed, as if preparing to answer her call.

"I want you…" She pouted her lower lip out. "To teach me how to read."

She what? He retreated another step. She was staying close, probably hoping to catch him off guard, and he'd use it to draw her out of his chamber.

But the wicked demon didn't take the bait. She propped an arm on the doorframe and rested her other hand on her generous hip.

Demon balls, he wanted to look so badly. "Why me?"

"I don't know many other demons who can do more than chisel their name, followed by 'was here' on the cave walls."

One would think she knew how to read from her state-ment, but she was older than him and incredibly astute. He gathered that when she went into the human realm, she absorbed information like an exotic sponge. It made sense. Her powers were attuned to the fear motivating other's actions, but he doubted she relied on her special ability alone. She read body language, listened to conversations, heard what wasn't being said.

And she spoke the truth. Hieroglyphs were popular in the underworld. Pictures told a story better and faster, especially for a population that didn't always share the same language or value reading skills. It was hard to when their leaders discouraged such communication. Anything to wall off power and maintain ignorance.

Learning his letters and numbers was one of the few good things his mother had passed down to him, and it'd only been to build him up to take over the underworld. She'd been so full of knowledge during her lucid moments, and so much hate otherwise, until her painful death. The older he'd gotten, the more she'd tried to kill him out of sheer bitterness.

"There are other demons who can read." He wouldn't have hoarded an extensive library if at least some demons didn't prefer to pen their ponderings and ambitions. "Why me?"

She cocked her head and gave him the most real look he'd seen from her yet. "Because you wouldn't demand my body or lewd favors in exchange."

Her confession rocked him. Again, she was correct. The underworld was brutal in its negotiations, a *what can you do for me?* realm. Many creatures didn't wait to take what they wanted, and many died trying. But if Xan asked for a favor, most would be damn sure to capitalize on the request. The greater the need, the more she'd be abused.

Which made his refusal easy. He didn't need anything from her and his conscience wouldn't suffer. She didn't need to read to thrive. Not his Xan— Not *Xan*. Just plain Xan.

She wasn't plain, but he couldn't argue with himself. He

27

had to get her out of his chamber. His ability to think and plot suffered when she was around.

"No."

Her brows popped up. Genuine surprise. He was getting all sorts of the real Xan. "No? Why the hell not?"

"I don't have time. And I don't need anything from you."

"Quution." She sauntered closer. He retreated until his back hit the wall across from his door. "Q. Are you sure you don't need anything from me? What if I'm willing to offer?"

His heart rate kicked up. "N-no."

Her breasts brushed his arm. He tensed every muscle in his body to keep from shaking. The staggering desire raging through him made him weak.

"I'm sure there's something you need from me," she crooned. "Down here, all by yourself. Doesn't it get lonely?"

His nostrils flared from the effort of holding himself still. Moments like this brought the horrible realization that he was nothing but a baseless demon at heart. A simple grab and turn and he'd have her pinned against the wall.

Prove you're not worthless, whelp.

His mother's sneer ricocheted around his brain, bringing him relief from his struggle. He was not a brainless creature. He would act around Xan like he acted around others. His lust was nothing but another emotion to manage.

"Why, yes, Xan. You do have something I want."

A delicate brow arched. Glow from the torches lining the corridor shimmered in the dark pools of her eyes. "Say it," she said, and it was too damn erotic.

"Tell me why you suddenly need to read. And who you work for, and why he or she sent you to spy on me."

She stiffened and withdrew, leaving a chasm of cool air wafting between them. "What the hell are you talking about?" In a heartbeat, her expression turned aloof.

As if she didn't know what he meant. "You've been

lurking around me, asking seemingly pointless questions. But you don't do anything without reason, nothing without benefit to yourself or your master."

At the word "master," a wave of murder rippled through her eyes.

He couldn't bring himself to be smug. It had been a bluff, but a fruitful one. Another demon controlled her. How? What vulnerability did Xan have that could be used to make her someone's marionette? She was the type of female who'd die for what she believed in.

And she was still alive because she believed in very little.

"So, when you come ready to exchange information for reading lessons, let me know." He sidled around her, darted into his cave, and slammed the door behind him. Energy shimmered as he wove it around the door. Forget deadbolts. He formed a shield against the stunned—and pissed-off—female outside his door.

CHAPTER 4

*I*t had taken all night to calm herself after
Quution's complete rejection.

That devious bastard. He knew she was up to something. Why couldn't he be a mindless male ready to mount her like so many others?

She'd gotten to him. His desire scared him. For a few blissful seconds, he'd dropped his guard and she'd sensed his fear.

He was terrified of losing control. The lust she'd incited bothered him deeply. It wasn't just that he wanted to fuck her, he was afraid of the innate vulnerability fucking required. He hated being enclosed in tight spaces, but at the same time space and freedom scared him.

So many secrets. She'd only tasted them. To her, they were like the candy beetles in the underworld. Sweet little treats with a satisfying crunch. Quution was full of them.

Ferreting out what he was up to regarding the underworld would take patience and a light touch. The other parts of himself he was hiding might be more attainable.

She started with what she knew about Quution.

His servant was another energy demon, Stryke. He was like the rock star of half-breeds, swoon worthy enough to make full-bloods want him. The last demon who'd tried to bend him to her will had failed so epically, she was dead now and her powers had been co-opted by a human—a former human, at any rate.

Stryke's sire was a notorious half-breed, a guy who'd duped the Circle about his status as a full-blood and attained a spot. The first ever half-breed on the Circle. At the time, it'd been unthinkable.

Energy demons were unusually uncommon. Was it possible they were related? Had someone in Quution's genetic pool dabbled with a half-breed? Unless it was him personally, it wouldn't do her any good.

I'm disappointed in myself.

What would Xera say? *Tweak your purple bits and get it together, Xan.*

She paced her chamber. Okay, what else?

He hung out with vampires. Those vampires had caused trouble in the underworld. She stopped and scrutinized the floor at the tip of her sharp toenails. Where had the vampires been down here? How could she find out?

If she were Quution, she could trace their energy signatures.

She racked her brain for the name of the demon Stryke had skewered. Herpes? Hanta? Hypna. That was it. Her chamber was a maze away, but it was a place to start.

Xan wove through the interconnecting corridors. Everlasting torches lit the way. The time of day didn't matter down here.

The stench of rotten flesh reached her before she turned a corner. Three forms huddled over a kill.

Another demon? Probably a halfling like her, killed by halflings like her, though these three were far down any evolutionary chain the underworld possessed. They probably didn't know who she was, and if they did, they wouldn't care. Food was their one and only goal.

She wasn't cannibalistic like many of her kind. But if she didn't tread cautiously, she'd become somebody's dinner. Stay vigilant, stay alive. She'd hate to go down as the Circle member who became dessert because she stopped and sniffed the candy beetles.

Damn, they were blocking her way. All three demons had black, stubby horns sticking out of their scalp and patches of hair covering their bodies. Two men, judging from the lump of dangling flesh between their legs. And a woman, who'd pierced both her nipples and used a hunk of rock like the ear plugs humans wore. The being they feasted on—well, it was impossible to tell now.

"Just gotta get around ya here." She calculated her path through them.

The female chortled and eyed Xan like she was the second course. "Looks like we get dessert, boys."

Rising to a stooped position, the males sniffed. Or was that a chuckle? The gurgle made it hard to tell. And disgusting. But they hunched farther over their food like they feared she'd take it away. The ever-present terror that they'd starve rolled off them.

An odd concern for a cannibal who lived among its food source. She tilted her head as they shuffled toward her. Uncoordinated. Lumbering. Disorganized.

Ah. Shitty predators. Their food usually outran or outsmarted them. What a coincidence. That was just what she'd planned to do. She'd been fooling cannibals since she was able to spit.

She called on her powers. Would they ever get enough to

eat? What if there was easy prey nearby? She gave them the impression that there were two young demonlings, lost and scared behind her a few turns. With short little legs, how could those poor young run away?

Then Xan threw in the suggestion that if the three lingered with her, they risked the mama finding her babies. No more vulnerable, tasty buffet.

The female lurched away from the pack to pass Xan and get at the fake food source. Xan's lips twitched. The weaker the mind, the more impressionable it was.

Peering beyond Xan, the males had already dismissed her as nothing. Ducking around them, she nodded to the female as she passed.

The pace of the shuffling changed, dirt crunching under someone's foot. Alarm bells blared in her mind. Xan spun around. The female lunged for her. Xan kicked her foot square in the demon's chest. The other female stumbled back and tripped over her roadkill. Broken from their trance, the males rushed to aid their companion.

Lowering into to a crouch, Xan sent another image: the fictional demonlings heard their mama and were getting farther away.

Desperate for easier prey than one they'd have to fight, the three snarled at her once then ambled down the hall. Xan straightened. Once the halflings disappeared around a corner, she cursed herself. What had happened to staying vigilant? A good reminder not to get too cocky. She'd dismissed them as mindless and could've ended up on the menu when she'd sworn not to let the Circle business go to her head. She had to watch her back now more than ever— she wasn't anonymous anymore.

It'd do her family no good to get dusted before she saved them. But after that, she'd have to figure out how to tell the Circle to take this damn position and suck it.

Rarely did she have to engage in physical fighting, and she hated unnecessary killing. But she was damn good at it. She could spin in midair and take out two targets, each one with a kick to the head. She could flip and twist, breaking bones and ultimately her target's will. She healed so quickly that if her adversary had a weapon, it was a minor inconvenience.

Xera was even better than her in a physical fight.

Xan still couldn't make sense of how Spaeth had caught Xera. The only thing that made any sense was Xoda. Spaeth must've gotten hold of her niece and coerced Xera the same way he had Xan.

Her search for Quution's weakness would kill two scavenger beetles with one heel stomp. He gave her a valid reason to hunt the underworld without Spaeth realizing she was stalking him too.

She slowed as she reached Hypna's old lair. Dying vines hung on the walls, and the floor was crusted over with old blood. Xan didn't have to be a total empath to shudder at the terror seeped into the walls. If this room were in the human world, it'd have all those paranormal hunters camped out inside. Bad vibes to say the least. Hypna had tormented several demons in this space.

Xan waited a moment as if information were going to jump out at her. There was plenty of fear stamped into the walls, but it was a jumbled mess. Other emotions, probably lust and greed, and of course terror, clogged the fear.

Frustrated, Xan stomped into the room. Hypna had been up to more than simple torture for pleasure in her chamber. The vampires had hunted her down for a reason and not just to keep Stryke from her toxic clutches.

Carvings caught her eye.

Xan knelt at one wall and cleared away the vines, which crackled and disintegrated like a withered bouquet. The wall wasn't smooth. Chunks had been gouged out. Epic tantrum, or a victim trying to escape?

Xan shrugged. Neither one helped her. She went to the other wall. Bits of old leaves flittered to the floor as she tugged vegetation out of her way. She crinkled her nose at the musty smell that rose when she handled the dying shrubbery.

The third wall was a bust. Same with the fourth.

Dammit.

She spun, her foot catching in old vines that pulled away from a rock, revealing a squiggly line beneath. Xan crept closer.

"Gross." Shards of fingernails and claws littered the floor and had collected in the corner over time. Hypna hadn't been a fan of housecleaning. She peered closer. They weren't all from the same being. She studied the dried twines with a different eye.

Bindings. Hypna had imprisoned her victims until she'd been done playing with them.

She turned her attention back to the squiggly line. It was so low to the floor. Given the homemade restraints Hypna had been capable of summoning, the line had to be from one of her unfortunate dates and not her. The longer Xan looked, the more squiggles she found—and the more deliberate they seemed. At one end was a stick figure with long horns—Hypna, obviously—and she held a small stick bundle over her head. The bundle, too, had tiny horns. Hypna with a baby? Hypna with someone else's baby?

Xan traced the line with her finger. A path. The rounded turns resembled the maze of the underworld. It wasn't pointing to any one place. It was just some poor, suffering being's last chance to imprint itself on the realm. This demon had been mapping the underworld when it landed him or her in Hypna's clutches.

Using her forefinger to pierce her skin, she dipped her stout claw into the wound. She healed too quickly to carve the path into her arm, but blood became ink as she lined her arm with a copy of the wall map. There was one area of the drawing that called to her, a section of the underworld she'd never been to. Maybe it had to do with Quution, maybe not. Maybe it'd get her closer to finding her sister, maybe not.

Either way, it was her next stop.

QUUTION ADJUSTED HIS POSITION. He was sitting in a black SUV on the outer edges of the vampires' compound. To travel to the human realm in his own form, he had to be bonded to a being from this realm. Since he refused to sacrifice his precious bond in order to make travel between realms easier, he used human hosts instead.

Thanks to his energy abilities, he was able to choose hosts susceptible to his possession instead of convincing or tricking them into being a host via a series of incantations.

Why had he picked a host with a small bladder? He had to keep stopping his meeting with Demetrius every ten minutes to take a piss.

It was bad enough he kept distracting himself. If he didn't deliberately concentrate on Demetrius, his mind wandered back to Xan and how she'd rimmed the tip of the scroll with one elegant finger. Regressing back to his formative years, he let his imagination turn the scroll into his dick.

"Q? Dude?" Demetrius snapped his fingers. "You gotta take another leak?"

Quution smiled tightly, vowing never to use this middle-aged host again. "Apologies. I don't believe this host realizes he has developed diabetes." The illness was what had made the host an easy target, but disappearing into the tree line to whiz was a pain. He hopped out and found a place to do his business.

Refusing to let the delay go to waste, Quution spread out his senses, dulled as they were in a host. He listened for a change in the energy vibes around him. Strongly suspecting the compound was under surveillance, he never let his guard down when he came here.

But if they were being watched, no one was close. They certainly couldn't hear him discuss plans with Demetrius.

He treaded back to the SUV and got in. Demetrius handed him a bottle of sanitizer. The male had been around Quution long enough to know his quirks. Not washing his hands after peeing with someone else's genitals gave him hives.

"The Synod is on board," Demetrius explained. He was only one of the government panel that oversaw vampires and shifters, but he was also the only one Quution did business with. Bastian was a backup, but the fewer ears that heard plans spoken out loud, the better. "They want to know the spells that will erect the wards and seal off the underworld. They're too far removed from this type of power to trust the underworld with it." What Demetrius didn't say was that the Synod didn't entirely trust Quution with that power either.

"I'm still researching how the incantations and wards would work. And the know-how must be limited to me—for now," he added when Demetrius's gaze grew weary from being tugged in too many directions.

"Not even a loose outline?" Demetrius asked hopefully.

Quution shook his head. "They already want to kill me just because I'm me and it's the underworld. If this gets out…" He'd be hunted until the all-too-soon end of his days. Then who would the Synod get to do their dirty work in the underworld? Stryke and Melody were the only other options, and they had mates who would stand with them until the bloody end.

No, this was for Quution to do alone. He wasn't above duping his own kind for the sake of the human realm. Demons weren't born to work together.

"Worst-case scenario," Demetrius said. "All hell breaks loose, literally. The Circle finds out that you plan to eternally anchor them to the underworld. Then what?"

Then I die and that's the end of it.

"Some of the half-breeds will see the need, but I doubt they could overpower the rest of the greedy realm. Sure, maybe Stryke could do it, but then you're risking Zoey. And Melody can't, though she'd try. Then you're also adding Creed into the mix. Either risk me, or risk four others. Thus the need for secrecy. I just need to find the missing part of the binding spell." To ensure he could bind himself to this realm, or he'd be as imprisoned as the rest of them.

"I'll get them to understand," Demetrius said. "One way or another. My entire team trusts you, and that's the only reason they aren't waiting outside of this vehicle."

The Synod would just have to be patient. "The problems in this realm, they are getting worse?"

Demetrius's eyes darkened and he nodded. "It's ugly. We've found whole houses of vampires slaughtered; we suspect because they refused to host demons. Creed has set up surveillance on every rich vampire's home, we're sweeping the streets where half-breeds infect destitute humans like lice, and…we're fucking losing ground. They're insidious at best, outright homicidal at worst."

Right, time was of the essence. "I'd better return this body." After grabbing a bit to eat. The host's blood sugar was dropping and the nausea and spinning head wouldn't make further discussion comprehensible.

Demetrius handed over a vial and started the SUV. To

keep the spotlight off Quution, he'd been tasked with collecting hair or blood from Melody. A curly blond hair was coiled inside the container. Perfect.

Quution should've collected a drop of blood from Xan when she'd fought for her spot on the Circle, but he'd been mesmerized. She'd been a graceful fighter, and only one of her competitors had managed to shed blood. The droplet had been just as unique as the female, incandescent purple, and once dried it had resembled mother of pearl—just like the gemstone Xan was. But it'd gotten mingled in all the other blood and grit on the ground. He'd missed his chance. He couldn't miss another.

Except, he had. Turning her down may not have worked in his favor, but it had helped his sanity.

Exiting Demetrius's vehicle, Quution returned to the one he'd used to meet with the male. The drive back to Freemont was uneventful. Quution stared out the window and watched people go about their evening. Some walked arm in arm. His host lived in the suburbs and it was still early enough to see kids running inside from some unknown errand.

Quution envied them. What would it be like to live in ignorance, to have a demon drive right by and not know, not even think it was possible?

He'd leave his host and go back to his own dismal home. The human he'd possessed would find himself parked in a gas station parking lot, not remembering much of the last several hours. Most hosts knew they were being possessed, but Quution was able to hide himself and take over so completely he could save the humans any angst.

Quution parked at a gas station, went inside, and bought a package of trail mix. Back in the car, he munched on the snack as he sifted through his host's memories.

He had a wife. Kids. Feared for his health. Wanted to do better for them.

Quution popped a cashew in his mouth. Were they so much different? Quution wanted to do better for future generations of his kind, but most days it was hopeless. Cruelty was bred into them. There was a reason demons had been driven to a different realm. He couldn't allow that kind of mentality into the human realm. They already fought their own inner demons; they didn't need real demons too.

CHAPTER 5

*T*he gruesome sight before her was…

Xan's jaw was hanging open. She closed her mouth and held the torch up, all while wanting to extinguish it and run away from this place.

Skeletons. Little ones. *Piles* of them.

Acid clawed at her stomach lining. This was one of those places that would get her killed just for knowing about it.

The picture from Hypna's cave of the demon holding the little bundle was of a sacrifice. Xan couldn't read the writing on the wall, but the power and despair roiling through the chamber was clear.

Xan threaded through the piles and around makeshift alters. Claw marks marred the surface. Gouges from blades.

Did Quution know about this place?

He had to. Hypna hadn't been killed because she'd been trying to stop this practice. That female had been evil to the marrow. Sacrifices like this had probably been her idea of a Sunday fun day.

Did Spaeth know about this?

If he did, would it change her situation? Probably not.

This chamber was sealed so securely she could barely squirm through the wards. Getting into Quution's chambers hadn't been nearly as hard as getting inside here. These wards had been disrupted at some point, then patched up with even more juice. But her sense of weakness wasn't only for living beings, but also for their powers. A quirk she'd developed after Mama's death—perhaps if it had appeared earlier, she might not have gotten kicked out. Though, as she toed a tiny finger bone aside, at least her mother hadn't done this.

Sacrificing babies. Xan could extrapolate from there about the whys and hows. Her half-breed kind was still enslaved, though not as badly now that Melody had flaunted her way on to the Circle and halflings like Xan had seized vacated seats.

But even so, pure demons continued to enslave their own half-breeds, considering them disposable. Could some of them be turning her kind into baby factories, using the babies to harvest power? She blew out a breath and skimmed her hand over her scalp. Was Spaeth using her sister like this?

The demon who had scrawled the map on Hypna's wall must've found this place and either been discovered by her or turned over to her. Was the map on the wall a last "fuck you" to Hypna? It'd been scratched in a hidden spot. Perhaps a desperate attempt to out the evil practice? Whatever the reason, she was grateful.

There were no clues as to Xera's whereabouts and Xan didn't detect her presence, despite scouring this part of the underworld for it. But this hell was never-ending.

She shook her head. If only this place were the worst she'd seen. Had whatever Quution and his brother done to Hypna stopped these heinous acts? Just delayed them, most likely.

Xan wiggled her way out of the chamber. Anyone who happened upon her would think she was a contortionist. It helped to move through the wards where power was the lowest, and sometimes that required acrobatics. The rest was just simple manipulation, which she'd worked hard to master.

Once clear, she didn't return to her own place. On the way to the hidden altar room, she'd sensed the subtle vibration of wards echoing down the chamber. Traces of her sister weren't in them, but Xan seemed to have a special receptor for Quution's powers.

She grabbed her torch and followed the path.

Lingering fear tickled along her skin. Definitely Quution's touch.

She shivered. A moan almost slipped out. Every time she was around him, he got better looking and she didn't think those words had ever been used to describe him. But his horns were a resplendent model of a summer sunset, the oranges gradually fading into his dark hair. And his eyes. So much depth holding back those delicious secrets.

The lips behind his garish fangs were lush, and damn if the fullness of his lower lip didn't give his mouth the shape of a heart.

His even shoulders were hitched, but they were broad. Something a girl could really hang on to.

She shook herself. Her infatuation with the demon was perplexing. He was a job; he couldn't be more.

He didn't want to be more.

Doing what she did best, she followed his lingering trail, pieces of himself he'd left behind that evidenced his weakness. They called to her power. The vibrations got stronger as she advanced.

Massive orgies or birthday parties could've been held here, but without the stench of fear, this passage would be nothing but empty to her stunted senses. The happy times experienced here would be lost on her. But after a few centuries, Xan had finely honed her skills despite her lack of the full range of empathic abilities.

Xan sensed fear around her as easily as she breathed, and it didn't matter where she was. If she'd ever interacted with the being the fear belonged to, she already knew their scent and could sift through it to look for causes, motives, and, most importantly, what in the world they would give to be rid of their fear.

She stalled. This space made him vulnerable. The wards were run-of-the-mill and wouldn't stop her anyway, but what she'd sensed from him earlier, combined with the hints of weakness in the wards—this place hurt him. Scared him. Had made him seal it against prying eyes. And she was so good at prying.

Following the maze, she came up against a rock wall.

"What the hell." She did not come all this way to hit a dead end.

She spun around, casting light on all the walls. Nothing.

But there was something. A place that was so dark her light couldn't penetrate. A smug smile curved her lips. At the bottom of the dead end, concealed where the darkness was the thickest, was a small opening.

She anchored her torch, wishing she hadn't used one, and let her vision grow accustomed to the darkness. But she heard nothing and sensed less.

Wedging into the opening, she wormed her way inside. It angled downward. Skittering in the walls surrounded her, faint but persistent. Ugh, the bugs were everywhere down here.

Which made any place in the underworld inhabitable. Even this dank space had a significant food source.

She slithered until the passage angled downward sharp enough to send her sliding.

Clawing for purchase, she failed and fell at least eight feet down. Her torchlight wouldn't reach down here.

Blinking, she waited for her night vision to strengthen. Shapes emerged. One large shape.

Bars, but carved from a single stone to make the gate of a prison cell.

Was Xera being held in a place like this?

And Xoda. Xan missed her laugh. So much like her sister, it was like a young Xera wandering around.

She couldn't sense her family or Spaeth. But Quution's fear ran rampant in this place. Xan soaked it in.

So much fear. But why?

Well, it was a prison. Had he been the prisoner? Her eyes finally adjusted to the dim space, but it was like looking at a world painted in dark grays. She slipped inside the cell.

The feeling of Quution surrounded her. He'd lived here. He had to have. Not even his current chamber resonated with so much of him.

She stepped back, her heel landing on a brittle bone. A scream stuck in her throat. She refused to let the sound out. She was not a demon who got rattled.

Sucking in a calming breath, she studied the bones. A skeleton. Someone full grown. Had this demon lived here too? At the same time as Quution? A toilet hole was in the corner, but its contents had long been scoured out by scavenger beetles. She feathered her hands along the wall. Symbols. Were they letters? Words? The ceiling and floor were covered with them.

Books were piled in the corner. Haphazard piles succumbing to gravity. This had to be Quution's doing.

Except he wasn't a willy-nilly guy. Those stacks would be neat and orderly. She padded toward the pile. She couldn't picture him having access to this pile and not reading each and every one.

She didn't know how old he was, but he had to be much younger than her. His appearance in the underworld was fairly recent. Like he'd just popped up out of nowhere, wielding his energy like a boss and disrupting their assumptions of how the underworld worked. When Melody had killed a particularly vicious Circle member and taken her seat, Quution's defense of her had been a potent demonstration that full-breeds didn't always hold all the power, a demonstration he'd pounded home by aiding even more half-breeds onto the Circle. A weird stance for a full-blood to take, but all the more effective because of his status.

She was nearly certain she'd solved the question of where he'd been until his first appearance. And since no one else knew, it had to be a helluva secret.

The skeleton—his keeper or another prisoner? A parent?

She might not have all the answers. But she had enough to bribe Quution to keep her nice and close. Or—her gaze flicked to the hole in the ceiling she'd been dumped from— she would once she clawed her way back out of here.

QUUTION NESTLED into the feather mattress on his stone slab of a bed. Other demons might see it as a weakness, but they'd never slept on a pillowtop Sealy. He was tempted to shuttle one down, but for now, his current mattress would have to suffice.

He hadn't seen Xan since he'd returned. That was good.

At leaste he kept telling himself it was. It didn't stop him from looking around each corner for the vexing female.

Teach me how to read.

He closed his eyes, dreaming of the day he could sleep without the fangs. After all these years, he should be accustomed to them, but they chapped his lips and he always woke up in a puddle of drool. His horns tucked in nice and tight against his hair, but the shoes were a pain. He couldn't risk taking them off and letting the underworld view the healthy, humanoid feet attached to equal-length legs.

He'd committed to the elaborate ruse. Just a while longer.

His eyes drifted shut, a to-do list streaming through his mind. He needed samples from two more Circle members. Xan would be tricky enough, but Spaeth—could Quution trap some of the male's radiation in an object? Would that be enough, or did the item have to be organic?

He couldn't risk it. Only a physical part of the demon would do.

Then he had to…

Sleep claimed him, deeper than it ever had before.

When morning came around, the most delicious scent tickled his nose. Had he just been dreaming about running through a field? The scent hadn't been wildflowers, it'd been…lavender, but that wasn't completely correct.

He popped an eye open and jolted. Xan was stretched out on her side next to him with her head propped in one hand.

He flipped backward, rolling off the slab. "What the hell are you doing here?"

Xan peered over the edge. "Good morning." She rested her chin on her hands. Lying on her belly, she was touching every part of his bedding. There was no laundromat in the underworld. He'd either have to possess a human to get some sleep or slumber while wrapped in her scent.

No. Just no.

Already, his body was awakening to the fact that a lovely female was naked in his bed.

"Get out," he said through clenched teeth, refraining from scooting backward across his floor like a damn coward.

"Mmm, no. We have a reading lesson to start."

"I said no."

"Oh, but see now I have something you want. Or should I say, I know something you want to stay secret."

Had she seen under his shirt to the unblemished skin underneath? Was the seam where his fake fangs were glued to his teeth visible? Had he talked in his sleep?

"How long have you been here?"

"I would've gotten here sooner, but…" Her face filled with annoyance, and swirls of lavender raced up and down her neck. A slow smile spread across the lips he tried hard not to fantasize about. "But you know how treacherous the path is from your childhood home."

Cold washed over him from horns to toes. His world stilled. She was bluffing. No one knew where he'd grown up, or how. Only Stryke. His brother had been through the same conditions.

"Who'd the bones belong to?"

Brimstone and fiery hell, she might not be bluffing. "What bones?" he hedged.

"See, I've been thinking. You and Stryke are buddies. You have the same colored eyes. Similar shades of hair. You're both energy demons."

His lungs froze as he waited for her to work out that, like Stryke's father, he might be hiding that he was a half-breed.

"And if I squint *really* hard and tilt my head, you two kind of resemble each other—in the face."

He ignored her dig about his body. He should be proud that his appearance had fooled her. But it wasn't the real him. The real him might repulse her. She went for fearsome demons. Even those former lovers who were humanoid like him had characteristics that struck fear into the beholder. His real fangs weren't much longer than hers, and except for his horns, he'd pass for a tall human man. He was basically a vampire with horns that could manipulate energy. That was all he was.

48

A rat with bones sticking out of his head, his mother had often said. The demon whose bones Xan had asked about.

"Stryke works for me," Quution said.

"Does he now? You know, I heard this tale once. His mother was a pure-blood demon, an energy one. However, plot twist: his sire was not. His father only *pretended* to be a full-blooded demon to secure a position on the Circle." Her feet kicked in the air as she talked, hanging out on *his* bed.

Like a fucking slumber party.

"Word in the corridors is that Stryke was kept secret. Because how in the world could a full-blood and another full-blood have a half-breed? Stryke's existence only confirmed his sire's half-breed status. But you know what I think? You two share a mother."

Quution's mind cranked. Xan hadn't guessed that he and Stryke shared *both* parents. He could deny it until his fake fangs fell out, but sometimes partial truths worked better.

"Those bones you asked about?" he said. "Our mother."

"Scandalous. Your sire?"

"An asshole." He wasn't lying.

"Mm. So why the prison?"

"Mother had bad taste in males."

"There's a good choice down here?"

Too true. "So that's why you snuck into my room? You'll tell everyone Stryke and I are half-brothers if I don't teach you how to read?"

"Isn't that enough?"

Did she know more? Dare he push and find out? The time it took to teach her how to read would be enough for him to determine the extent of her knowledge while keeping others from learning the real nature of his relationship with Stryke. It wasn't hard to make the jump that they were full brothers and Quution was a half-breed. And if that happened, he'd lose all credibility and be more hunted than he already was.

But if he played along, would Xan figure it out?

He'd have to keep her close to know. "Fine. Our lessons start this afternoon."

"Got plans this morning?"

"I can't teach you with these tomes. They're too complicated, and carving into stone is too time-consuming. I'll go topside and gather supplies."

"Let me go with you." Xan pushed herself up on her arms, her breasts swaying.

He tore his gaze away. "I can't wait for you to find a host."

"I have one." She rattled off an address. "Pick me up there in an hour."

He could argue, but seeing the host she chose and the way she acted in the human realm would tell him a lot about her. And they'd both be possessing a human. He'd choose a woman; that way they would be on equal footing.

If there even was such a thing with Xan.

CHAPTER 6

*T*he search for a female host went faster than Quution had anticipated. He closed his eyes and zoned in on a college campus. Easy targets. The uncertainty of gainful employment after sinking massive amounts of money into an education made some students a mess of anxiety, their personal energy churning in one area of their brain. It left their psyche vulnerable. He could latch on to the energy pattern and squeeze his way inside.

He drove to the address Xan had given him. She had sprinted from his place as if worried that one more second in his bed would be long enough for him to change his mind.

She didn't realize the secret she was sitting on was enough to destroy everything he'd worked for his whole life. He'd jump on one foot and yip like a Chihuahua if she asked.

Shifting in his seat, he marveled over the comfort of the host's clothes. Black leggings and a college sweatshirt. Her bra pinched the sides of her ribs, but there was no waistband digging into her belly, no gaudy belt chafing her skin. The shoes were…what were they called? Ah yes. Ballet flats.

Comfortable. He should possess college students more often.

The car was a sturdy little sedan without a speck of dust. Her purse was meticulously organized. His host was obsessive. No wonder her mess of an energy pattern had called to him.

Arriving at a sprawling apartment complex, he slowed and pulled into the parking lot. Xan said she'd be by the south door, but all he saw was a large man perched on the bottom step.

The man's dark gaze tracked him and Quution's stomach sank. He should've expected that she'd find a host similar to herself. Smooth scalp. His skin wasn't purple, but it was dark, and his muscles nearly squeezed out of the sleeves of his white tee. A man in his prime, just like Xan was in hers.

A man who would tower over his five-foot-three-inch host.

Equal footing his ass. How'd Xan always manage to keep the upper hand?

He pulled up in front of the man and rolled down the window.

"I'd recognize you anywhere," he said drily.

"Nice specimen, isn't he?" The low rumble was so unlike Xan's husky voice, but the cadence was right. The man's chin lifted. "She's cute."

To another, perhaps. To him, the hair was too distracting, the eyes too bright, and the skin too pale. But maybe she didn't blackmail her partners, either.

"Get in, Xan."

"It's Marcus," Xan said as she slid in.

"I didn't get my host's name." It was Brooklyn.

Xan flipped open the glove compartment and rustled through papers. She held up the car registration. Damn her and her quick thinking.

He didn't have to read the name printed on the card. He already knew. "Brooklyn Russo," he gritted out.

Xan's self-satisfied smile was irritating as she stuffed everything back in a way that would drive his host nuts. "So, Brookie. Where are we going?"

"To the dollar store."

"Way to go all out."

He slid his gaze to her. "I don't like to needlessly siphon off my host. And the dollar store has an incredible write-and-wipe board selection and cheap markers. Also flash cards and kid books."

She bristled at the word "kid." Only when Marcus bristled, he took up half the car.

"Your host works out." He changed the subject before she could dwell too much on his choice of teaching tools.

"Obsessively. I guess he grew up scrawny and got picked on."

"Does he own the gym?"

"No, he's an insurance agent. Between his insecurity and his crazy ex-girlfriend, I was able to get him to recite the incantation. He would've done anything for her. The fool believed in true love—you know, that bullshit humans fall for. What's yours do?" Xan lifted a dark brow and eyed the petite host. "Or is she still in diapers?"

"She graduates college in the spring. Accounting."

"College girl. I expected a more complex target out of you."

"I use my energy efficiently."

Xan bought a soda at the dollar store. When Quution shot her a questioning look, she shrugged. "Marcus has gotta realize treating himself once in a while isn't going to kill him."

Shaking his head, he went through his items. Letter flash-cards. A set for numbers. Two write-and-wipe boards, one with lines for writing practice. And a pack of assorted markers.

"That's all we'll need," he said. "Apologies that it was no big mystery."

Xan drained her Coke, belched, and rummaged through the bag. She frowned at the kid book with balloons and a cat across the front. "Score one for Quution. This is insulting."

"It's not meant to be." His voice sounded so prissy coming from this host. "I've possessed teachers before and these are the types of books they start with."

The book got tossed back into the bag. "Teachers? Do you glean the careers from all your hosts?"

"I'm hungry for learning." What else was he going to do? If he didn't have plans for the underworld, he'd spend all his time in hosts.

Xan folded her host's arms. The man's muscles were intimidating, even to a guy like himself. "What are you getting from the accountant?"

"I can list the types of expenses Marcus can deduct for his insurance business."

"Mm."

She did that a lot. A simple acknowledgment of what he said, neither agreeing nor disagreeing but still giving him the sense that she wasn't buying whatever he was selling.

"I'll drop you off and go park where I found this host. We'll meet back in my cavern. I trust you can get in with the wards up." He didn't bother to hide his annoyance. His wards worked on every being thus far but her.

"Why not study at Marcus's?"

"You want to learn to read at his place?"

She lifted a giant shoulder. "Why not? It's quiet and there are fewer spies around his apartment complex. I can't say the same for the university."

It was a good idea, but he hated disrupting his host's life

more than necessary. "I should get her back. Wasn't Marcus going to work or something?"

"He works from home. So he'll miss a few calls from an old lady wondering if her Medicare Plan A, B, C, or double-D will cover her meds."

"Sounds important for the lady."

Xan rolled her eyes. "Quution. He can call her back. Besides, he does most of his work in the morning and works out all afternoon. What was your host going to do?"

He checked his clothing. She'd been planning on going for a run, then cleaning her tiny apartment all day to avoid applying for jobs. He wouldn't be interfering in any life-changing events. "Fine. Marcus's place."

Xan wanted to stab the blunt marker into the hand of Quution's delicate host. It was like her own host had pheromone receptors just for this petite female and they were crossing over to Xan, making her horny and irritable. On top of her embarrassment at forgetting the order of the letters of the alphabet.

"Patience," Quution chided. "Learning to read takes time and I don't know if my methods suit your style."

"You mean my style isn't cutesy animals snaking over the letters?"

"Possibly. We're very similar to humans, not that any demon will admit it, so I think this will work. But you're thinking you can learn something in a few hours that takes humans a good decade or two to master."

"I'm not human," she bit out. She wasn't a male, either, but that didn't stop Marcus from sporting an erection whenever Brooklyn leaned over in her chair and flashed her shapely ass.

Quution sighed and pushed the write-and-wipe board in front of her. On it he'd written a single *A*. She was supposed to fill the board with *A*s. "As you pointed out, I was imprisoned most of my life, with nothing to do but read the books my mother was allowed to have. It took me many hours, every single day of my life, until I knew freedom."

And he hadn't stopped learning. What had happened to him down there had only created a tyrant with a dry eraser. He tapped the board with a shiny fingernail.

She growled at him, the sound so satisfying in Marcus's deep timber, and traced her first *A*. Holding the marker didn't feel as foreign as she'd feared. Marcus's hand adapted naturally even if his consciousness was suppressed. And she'd used enough knives and blades to do her dirty work over the centuries that she was nimble when it came to tools.

"After the human alphabet, are you going to teach me the demon languages?" She should've asked earlier, but she'd been too euphoric over having trapped him into a reason for spending hours upon hours with her.

"Most of our languages revolve around the human alphabet, English in particular. You'll find many of the tomes written in some form of English, though some are very Shakespearian."

She forced her voice to sound cultured. "Indeed."

As she mimicked his *A* for two more lines, his stare burned into her. She concentrated on her task. If he had something to say, he needed to come out with it.

"You think I'm arrogant," he finally said.

Why'd he care what she thought of him? "Yes. You're rather stuck-up. It's why all the Circle members hate you." She was exaggerating. Only half hated him. But she might be able to get him to confide in her.

"Not all of them."

"You mean Melody? She seems fond of you. Did you save her life?"

"She saved her own." He was quiet for a moment. "What do the others say?"

"Oh…" She had no idea. Fear demons weren't high on the social ladder. It didn't help that she embraced the distrust and outright hatred of her kind. A few comments and a couple of knowing looks, and her companion ended up crying or a mess of nerves. Her popularity was understandably low as a result. Especially after she'd so publicly destroyed her competition to get a seat on the Circle. Her stony competitor had been so afraid of heat and melting his rock-hard armor off that she'd convinced him to peel it off lest it trap him. When he'd gone running and screaming from the fight, she had smiled triumphantly, only to see horror on her spectators' faces. She could've beheaded the guy and they would've cheered, yet the prospect of losing face so publicly was anathema to them. "That you're planning to take over the underworld."

Inside his diminutive host, he recoiled, but she could imagine the real Q doing so too. "I have no wish to conquer anyone. I would love to make it a habitable place for all of us."

"You speak as if it's possible. Forget the hurdle that is every full-blood ever. Have you met some of the halflings?" She wrote her last *A* and pushed the board back to him. "Done."

Her writing was neat, if a bit wobbly. Good thing there wasn't a mirror around. She was probably beaming.

Quution gave one nod, then the bastard erased all her work. He outlined a *B* and slid it back to her.

Fucker. She stretched her hand, but the stiffness was in her imagination. Marcus was as used to wielding a pen as he was a barbell.

"Why all the writing?" Was she whining? She hated whiners. "I asked to learn to read."

"It helps cement the language into your brain." He tapped the board.

"Do that one more time and I'm going to smash your finger into the table."

He was unruffled. Downright prissy in that host of his.

Did he like the pale look? Is that why he'd chosen Brooklyn? Was her small body more desirable? As if she could handle a male Quution's size. Her hand couldn't even wrap around one of his horns and give it a good stroke.

Marcus's body suddenly grew hot and restrictive. She shifted in her chair, one second away from darting out the door. But this was her host's home. And she had a string of *B*s to write.

"Can't I learn other letters while I'm doing this? This one-at-a-time bullshit seems horribly inefficient." She met his gaze and purred. "I know how you like efficiency."

Quution's lips parted. Xan almost grinned. She'd gotten to him. Under all those brains, he was a male.

She could use that.

He blinked and even through his host, Xan could see he was back to the impassive male he presented to everyone else. He started reciting the ABCs, differentiating between vowels and consonants while she traced letters.

By the end of the day, she could sing that ridiculous alphabet song and write every letter on command.

"We'll have to meet in the underworld to do this tomorrow," he said as he packed up. "We can meet—"

"At your place." Spaeth's spies needed something to spy on and it'd behoove her if they reported that she was spending time with Quution. "No one bothers you there."

"Only you."

"Aw, Quution." She patted the soft cheek of his host. "You say the sweetest things."

"How do you get in?"

"A girl never tells her secrets."

"She isn't the only one," he muttered.

We'll see about that.

CHAPTER 7

*H*e looked peaceful when he slept. Xan relaxed next to the big male on his stone slab. The whole mattress thing was nice. She'd been through all his possessions before and he stored quite the treasure trove. None of it told her anything about what he was up to that had Spaeth so worried.

The bedding was unique. Clothing. Human weapons. Those may be useful, but she'd made sure she could defend herself with nothing but her fists and her mind.

She scanned his form as he slumbered next to her. Why the clothing?

Everyone, repeat, everyone was nude in the underworld, except the new demon, Melody. But even that female wove vines over herself, not clothing. Over the centuries, many items from the human world had found their way down here. Usually it happened when a host died and a portal opened to suck the demon back home. Collateral damage. But every item that had fallen down here was precious and hoarded—not worn for all to see.

Quution had a purpose for everything, and his penchant

for clothing was about more than advertising his energy abilities. So why the clothing? Xan lifted her gaze to peer down his shirt. It was skintight, and the vexing male wore that atrocious trench coat to bed, too. She rolled back slightly to see if there was a gap at his waistband.

Cinched tight.

What was he hiding? She studied his skin. His face was smooth, the tone swarthy, like he'd spent a lot of time in the sun. Her fingers twitched to feather over his face, across his cheeks to outline his chiseled bone structure. The cleft in his chin was mesmerizing—and amazingly visible between his shanks for fangs.

She scowled at the fangs, wishing she could see his lips without the hindrance of his ivory. They were odd looking. She couldn't imagine them holding up while ripping into flesh, but Quution wasn't a flesh-ripping demon. He liked subterfuge, maximizing efficiency, and saving the dirty work for others.

Her gaze traveled down his neck. Smooth. She frowned and tilted her head. His shoulders were even as he rested. When he stood and walked, one hitched much higher than the other and threw his entire gait off. The fighter in her noticed those traits in others. Lying flat, he was even. Proportional. A lot like Stryke.

Something was off about Quution.

His eyelids floated open. She was pinned under his lilac stare. His nostrils flared like he was smelling her, but he didn't start like he had the day before. Hopefully, their time together would make him more comfortable around her. So he would tell her all his secrets and she would free her sister.

"How the hell do you keep getting in here?" His sleep-roughened voice zinged straight to her belly. A familiar warmth curled through her. It wasn't purely sexual, and that was disturbing. His epic patience yesterday had been endearing. It was an unusual trait in demons and one she used to scorn, but in him, she liked it.

As for his question—getting in was easier than ever. Almost as if his energy were parting just for her. Soon, she'd be able to wander right in like she lived here.

"Tricks of the trade."

His lips flattened as much as they could and he rolled up to a seat. "Have you eaten yet?"

"Munched a few candy beetles on my way here." It was almost all she ate.

"I have some trail mix." He reached under his stone slab into a compartment she hadn't seen before and retrieved a bag of nuts and raisins.

She sat up. His broad back was to her and again his shoulders were aligned. "You can smuggle anything down here and you pick that atrocious mix?"

He glanced over his shoulder, the move making his horns shimmer like they had their own light. The color blazed like the torches lining the wall. "What would you have me bring?"

She rolled to her knees to get a closer look at each horn. They curved elegantly and the orange shimmer... "Do your horns glow?"

"They can if I want them to."

"You can control it?" She lifted a hand to touch them.

"It's all energy."

She snatched her hand back. What was she thinking? Stroking Quution.

Xan changed the subject. "I'd bring some of the good stuff down, like cheesecake. You want nuts? At least get ones covered in chocolate."

"I don't care for sweets."

Further proof she needed to keep her hands to herself. She could succeed without seducing him. "Monster."

He chuckled, an honest, very male sound that made her

belly flip. "I don't care for them as my main form of sustenance."

"You should. Life's too short to eat bland food. Or scavenger beetles."

His heavy shoulders shuddered. "If I never eat one again, I'll be happy." He held out the bag of trail mix. She plucked out a raisin. It would have to do.

Swallowing she asked, "Where do we start?"

QUUTION NODDED as Xan nailed another word. He'd have to make a run to the human realm to gather more books. Xan was a fast learner, as he suspected she would be. At this rate, she'd be reading everything in his library by next week.

Grammar was likely to make her cranky. She didn't seem one for rules. Rules were made to be bent to Xan's will.

Sometimes when she was around, like this morning when he'd first woken up, he almost thought she was attracted to him. Her gaze kept straying to his horns and his body reacted by sending blood to his groin instead of his brain.

Sweet brimstone, the morning had been painful. As long as they were deep in concentration, he could pretend she wasn't nude and keep his roaming gaze upward. Xan didn't seem to have such trouble while working. Her eyes were on the book.

What did it matter if she was interested? It wasn't like he could strip down in front of her and explain why he appeared to be a half-breed.

When he chose to finally sleep with someone, he'd need their full trust. Xan wasn't here learning to read because she was trustworthy.

"The...dog...sat..." Her brow crinkled as she puzzled over the last word. "D-down."

"Good."

The wiggle in her seat she gave whenever he praised her would be his undoing. He'd compliment her for the rest of his life to see that shimmy.

"That's all we have for today," he said. "I'll grab more books before our lesson tomorrow."

"Why can't we use the books you have in your library?"

Because he needed a break to rebuild his restraint. He'd been fighting off an erection for hours. It taxed his mental acuity and she was a distraction. "I have work to do."

She leaned toward him. "Secret Circle work?"

He sucked in a breath. She might have broken in to his place and blackmailed him into these lessons, but he would not sport a hard-on around her like a bull in heat. "If it were Circle work, you'd know about it, since you're on the Circle."

"Come on, Quution. Do you think I'm that clueless? Each member has secret Circle work."

He pounced on the opening. "What's yours then?"

Her eyes widened briefly, but she recovered. "Learning. I don't worry about a physical altercation, but there are several ways to build my defenses."

"Likewise."

She swirled on the boulder to face him. Had she purposely sat with her legs open? Lavender-laced brimstone surrounded him and it sapped even more of his strength not to leer at her body.

She walked her fingers over his chest.

He made a strangled sound and lurched sideways to leave, but her leg blocked him in. Dammit. He'd have to push her out of the way or hop over her. Either choice and she'd know how much she affected him.

"Can I practice reading while you're studying in the library?"

There was no reason she couldn't. Except that he couldn't think with her in the same room.

"You'd break my concentration by continuously asking for help."

Her eyes narrowed and there was that damn guilt again. Yes, he'd said it to upset her, hoping she'd storm off again and give him breathing room. She did not like him alluding to her ignorance, and he'd abused that fact a few times already.

He hated himself for it.

Determination filled her features. "I promise not ask questions."

He sighed. She was going to continue until he said yes, or he feared she'd find another reason to make him say yes.

"Fine." The smile he was graced with put a lump in his throat. She was quite the alluring female. Too bad he was only a job to her.

She stood and motioned for him to lead the way to the library. Finally, a little space was between them.

As long as she was inviting herself along, he might as well make her recite her *ABC*s and spell out simple words on the way. She cut off at *M* to grab a candy beetle and munch on it.

"This one's ripe. Have a taste." She held out the bug. Half the body was missing and two of its legs stuck in the air. His stomach turned.

"No, thank you."

"So proper," she muttered, then stopped. "*No way.* You don't eat any food from our realm?"

He clenched his jaw and kept walking. "No."

"You smuggle all your food down? Or do you hop into Brittany and grab a smackerel?"

"Brooklyn." As long as Xan thought he used Brooklyn as his only host, that was fine with him. He had no wish to be captured and tortured in order to stuff other demons inside

65

humans once it became common knowledge he didn't need his host to recite an incantation. "And yes, after years of scraping for even the stankest of bugs, I have no wish to ever sink a fang into one again."

"And you don't eat other demons. Mm." She popped the chunk of candy beetle into her mouth. "Seriously," she said around her food, "not even these little delights? I can rustle them up easy enough. I just make them think there's a predator behind them."

He felt for the beetle. He would rush toward Xan, too. "Do you eat other demons?" He thought he knew the answer, but really, he didn't know Xan that well at all.

"Not these days. Life was good for a while."

What did she mean by that?

"Anyway, there's nothing wrong with dessert for all three meals. Sometimes it's the only good part of the day." She shook herself like she realized she was sharing too much. "That's the underworld for you."

"Yes."

Life was good for a while. Was it not good for her anymore?

XAN'S BRAIN THROBBED. Maybe there was something to those kid books after all. She'd gotten through four pages in the last two hours. Some words she'd sounded out, but others were tongue twisters.

And no way was she interrupting Quution after what he'd said. Did he have his own ability to sense her weakness? Appearing inept around him certainly seemed to be it.

He was sitting at the desk behind her. He'd said he hadn't retrieved the desks or chairs from the human realm, but that they'd been items sucked in through a portal several years back. Her desk faced one wall and his faced the opposite. *A better atmosphere to study.*

Sure. He could keep telling himself that.

She turned around and peeked over his shoulder. Those broad shoulders were hunched over a scroll. The way he'd unrolled it with the gentlest of hands made her envious of the damn parchment. For a big demon with grotesque, twisted claws, he had a deft and considerate touch.

What was he like during sex? Demons fucked fast and hard, and often brutally. The males she'd been with had had only one goal in mind: to get off. Though she'd chosen partners who actually waited for her permission. All others had faced their demise before they could plunder any part of her.

But Quution. Deliberate, hulking, contemplative Quution.

She spun on her seat to stare at him. Her work for the day was done or her eyes would cross and she'd have to kill a demon for supper just to release her frustration.

She hadn't gleaned any new information from the male. He was closed down and blocked to her. She was exploiting one of his secrets—there was a biggie in there—but figuring it out was like slamming her body against a stone wall. Nothing. There was more to his capitulation than fear of his half-brother being exposed, something bigger than the dirt she'd sifted through on him.

It was time to ramp up her efforts.

He either hadn't noticed her looking at him, or he didn't care. She rose and sauntered around his desk.

He popped his head up, his shoulders tense.

Oh, he knew what she was up to. The question was, would he stop her?

"Quution." She dropped her voice to a seductive octave. "Doesn't sitting like this put a kink in your back?"

She clamped her hands down on his shoulders and squeezed. Damn, it was like trying to massage a brick.

Putting her mouth to his ear, she whispered, "Relax."

He didn't relax one millimeter. "What are you doing?"

"Releasing tension." She pinched his shoulders. Was that all muscle? Alternating squeezes, she moved her hands along his shoulders. Rock hard. Defined. This demon was sporting a hell of a physique.

He spun out of her grasp, his chair squeaking. Oh no, he wasn't getting away.

She twirled around him and plopped onto his lap. A little off-kilter, thanks to one of his legs being propped higher than the other. She scooted closer to him and gave in to her urge to stroke his horns.

His lips parted and he inhaled so slowly it had to border on painful.

"So soft," she breathed. Silk-covered steel ran under her fingers. She rimmed each horn from the sharp tip to the thick base buried in his rich hair.

His hair. Satiny strands wound through her fingers as she twisted and twirled her hand. She'd never been with someone who was such a mixture of hard and soft, each texture pleasing.

She trailed her fingers down his cheek. His eyelids slid closed as if her touch was the most exquisite sensation he'd ever felt.

Those fangs were growing on her. She touched the corner of his lips and skimmed her finger over a fang.

His eyes flew open, full of alarm. Strong hands clamped like shackles around her wrist.

Under her ass was another hard body part prodding her sex. She ground down, and he groaned, his eyes losing focus.

She rocked her hips again. Ooh, that was delicious.

His hands slipped off her wrists. She wrapped her arms around him and rode his erection.

A steel grip tightened on her waist. She ground down harder. But, oh, she needed more and he wasn't moving. His gaze was stuck on her breasts and it was the first time she could recall that he'd looked at them.

Arching her back, she stuck her chest out. She needed more.

With a growl, she wrenched his hand off her waist to shove it between her legs to her needy clit. He went even more rigid, and his claw grazed the sensitive flesh between her inner thighs.

She gasped from the shock of the scrape, the zing of pleasure-pain. Quution snapped his hand back and stood. She would've been dumped ungracefully off his lap, but his hands wrapped around her biceps like a steel band, yanking her to her feet.

She blinked, her head spinning for a few heartbeats as she reoriented herself. Her core throbbed with unrequited need. Quution's desire clogged her nose until she could roll in his firestorm scent. She'd tried to, but he'd dumped her off.

"Apologies. Did I hurt you?" He released an arm to glare at the offending claw.

"Is that why you stopped us before go time? It was just a little scratch." She rotated her leg out to look at the wound. "Don't you usually scratch and nibble during sex?"

Quution lurched away. He raised his hand like he was going to shove it through his hair but scowled at his claws again and clenched his fists at his side.

"We can't…" he huffed. "You can't…"

She watched him prowl the library, turning every which way that wasn't toward her. Didn't he find her attractive? "If you don't want to fuck, just say so."

He shook his head. "I can't…fuck…with you."

She rolled her eyes. His discomfort at talking about the subject was so innocent she could barely stand it. "Quution, you're like a Puritan girl before her wedding night." Xan shuddered. What a nightmare that had been. "You don't like me, just say so."

Her heart skipped a beat. He wasn't going to say it, was he? What did it matter? He was a job, a means to an end.

She'd become more attracted to him, not less. How could that be possible? He was so not her type. His brother might have been, before he'd become a vampire sympathizer, but not Quution.

She wasn't one willing to sleep her way to the top, since the top meant giving herself to full-bloods. They were violent and selfish in bed.

"We just can't. You can read." Quution cut a hand through the air. "Our bargain is done."

No, this couldn't be the end of their deal. Her dismay had nothing to do with facing Spaeth with no answers. She just didn't want to be done with Quution. He was a patient teacher and this reading business satisfied her natural curiosity without hurting anyone.

She adopted a haughty expression and scoffed. "So you're saying I can pick any book off this shelf and read it?"

Quution's gaze darted to the shelves.

Xan sauntered closer to his desk and plucked a scroll off. "And you're saying…" Damn, her ingenious idea of getting close to his reading material had failed. This was in another language.

He spun around, his arm twitching like he wanted to grab the scroll from her but had decided against revealing how important it was to him. He didn't want her reading it, she guessed. A dull glow warmed her belly. He thought she had progressed fast enough to adapt to a new language?

"Oh, look at that." Her gaze swept the contents, trying to

memorize the combination of letters and symbols. Pointless. "I can't read it."

She dropped it on the desktop like it was a bug below her concern.

"You only asked me to teach you to read. I taught you."

"Teach me more."

His lower lip puffed against his fangs. Her request troubled him. Was she that repulsive? Was someone like Brittany —Brooklyn—more his type? Did he have a human fetish? "I can teach you, but keep your hands to yourself."

Planting her hand on her hip, she sighed to cover her hurt feelings. "Surprise, demon. It won't be hard. You don't exactly inspire wild lust." Could he tell she was lying? At some point, he'd come to do nothing but inspire wild lust in her.

Hurt rippled across his features. Oh, her dismissal of him went too far, but he could demand she not lay one finger on him lest she pass on half-breed germs?

Arrogant ass. She spun on her heel and strode toward the exit. "Tomorrow. Your place."

It'd give her time to gather herself, nurse her pride, and steel herself to play aloof around him.

CHAPTER 8

The write-and-wipe board was full of words, sentences even. Xan had studied every night for the last week. She had to get started on new languages so she could decipher what Quution buried his long, straight nose in at his desk.

"So you can concentrate better," he'd said.

Mm. Getting close to him was proving harder than she'd ever anticipated. No wonder he'd risen to the top without leaving a mile-long trail of bodies behind him. He was smart, patient, and determined. When an opportunity presented itself, he made sure he was ready. He also did what he could to limit interference. Like he'd done in this cursed library.

She glared at Quution's broad back. "When can I learn another language?" He hadn't answered when she'd posed the question a couple of days ago.

"Quution." She tapped her foot impatiently and it was the only time she wished she wore shoes. Her bare foot slapping the ground wasn't nearly as intimidating.

"Soon," he grunted, bent over another damn scroll. "You need to write more."

"No. I don't. I have no plans to pen the next great master-piece of the underworld." Her plans included finding her sister and getting her far away from Spaeth. With her niece. "I want to read them." Just to satisfy her revenge craving, she dropped her voice a few octaves. "You know, for those times when I'm alone in my chamber, and I can't sleep. I'm just so…restless. And I have to do something with my hands. To relieve the pressure. Since I can't read, and I need to relax, I start by brushing my hand along my collar, drifting down-ward, over my breasts, and—" She gasped like she'd caught herself by surprise.

His shoulders stiffened and she grinned. Abandoning her chair, she padded toward him. This was the first opportunity she'd had in days to get close to those damn scrolls he hoarded like a dragon over its gems. She toed quietly his way. He had to know she was coming for him, but he was at the point where he could tell himself it wasn't happening.

And why? She'd never met a male—a demon no less—who'd pass up a quick fuck, a little study break that included penetration and climax. Fear of intimacy was his weakness, one she didn't care to exploit. An unusual trait for her, but in the past, those she'd targeted had deserved it. She had yet to get an inkling Quution had what was coming to him from Spaeth.

She was close enough to wallow in his firestorm scent. She'd never look at a fire the same way again. Walking her fingers along his shoulders, she smiled enough to reveal a fang when he jerked, still afraid to look at her.

Where had she been? Oh yes. She leaned down to speak into his ear, her breath tickling over his hair. "And over my stomach, down to my hot, wet—"

He exploded out of the chair, knocking her back. She recovered her balance, but dammit, he'd yanked the scroll off the desk before she could get a peek.

"You promised no touching. We're done for the day," he said, his voice shaky. He frantically rolled up the scroll, the jittering of the skin parchment sending dust flying off it. The scroll was so full of information, there was even writing scrawled across the outside. She could still save this day and get a tidbit to feed Spaeth with.

"Quution." She prowled toward him.

His exotic eyes widened.

"What's going on in that big brain of yours? I want you. You want me. Let's just do it."

His lips parted, and curse those fangs, she couldn't get a clear view of them.

"I can't…" His resolve was weakening.

She glided closer, her gaze on his lips and not the scrolls. His mouth mesmerized her as she planned how she could plant hers on top without getting a mouthful of fang.

A tingle started at the base of her brain. No. No, not now. Spaeth was demanding her attendance, and likely wanted a boatload of dirt she didn't have. She didn't even have a spoonful, except for the information about how he'd grown up and the chamber of doom she'd found. But she hadn't even gone after Quution for answers about the sacrifices. And her natural senses were telling her that she shouldn't mention a thing to Spaeth lest she end up in one of the bone dumps. And if she ended up there, Xera was soon to follow. And Xoda. Xan almost winced at forgetting her niece again.

She snapped her fingers. Quution jumped, his gaze jumping from her hand to her face. She didn't dare eye the scroll in his arms.

"You know what?" she said. "I forgot that Marcus has a massage today and I was going to jump on board. A girl's gotta have some me time."

Without explaining further, she pivoted and put on her sexiest sashay toward the door. His gaze burned into her back, between her shoulders. Again, he showed restraint. He could be staring at her ass instead, and she would've enjoyed it.

Weaving through the caverns, she took a few extra loops in case Quution or any other demons were following her. It served the dual purpose of cooling her body off. She'd been so close to kissing Quution. She had yet to plant a solid one on him. Last week, they'd only done a little bump and grind, emphasis on grind.

Which was fine. But what would kissing him be like?

"What took you so long?" Spaeth spat, a few droplets hitting her arm.

She bit back a hiss as his acid spit seared through her skin. She'd heal. "I was finally getting close. He's a smart one."

Spaeth appeared in front of her, his gaze shrewd. "I don't pay you for close."

You don't pay me at all. She had the good sense not to argue. "He's closeted. His nose is always buried in scrolls, but he hides them. I was an inch away…" *When you interrupted my chance to taste the male!*

"Xan. Are you failing to accept responsibility again? I find this unacceptable." Spaeth flashed behind her. "I'll be sure to let your sister know as she pays for your ineptitude."

She stiffened. If she was annoyed by a few drops of burning spit, what was her sister experiencing? Or Xoda?

"I'm protecting your identity." Xan tried not to sound desperate. "Quution is studying hard, still researching. He's not close to his goal." Whatever it was. "But I was under the impression that my mission was top secret. Quution's smart." Probably the smartest one down here. "He'll know if I push, and he'll find you."

Spaeth surged next to her ear. The tender skin of her lobe ached. Lesions spread down her neck. "You'd better make sure he's not. You want time?" he snapped.

MARIE JOHNSTON

She flinched. Droplets of spittle dotted her cheek and neck. The smell of her own skin burning made her stomach churn. It was nothing compared to her sister. Or her niece.

"One week, Xan." He said each word deliberately. "I want to know everything. Or you won't even find their rotting remains." He appeared long enough to lay a hand on her arm. She clenched her teeth but refused to cry out at the agony coursing over her skin.

"Yes, Spaeth." She hated being the obedient servant. The underworld had no currency. It wasn't like she could hire her abilities out. But she'd always had bargaining opportunities. Spaeth had taken that from her when he'd taken her family. Her family was his currency.

She took her time going back to her chamber. Her mind churned with a plan. Quution had let his fears seep out enough for her to have formed an idea for a hallucination based on his weakness. All she needed was a way to access him when he was most vulnerable, which she had. Watching him while he slept would be considered creepy in any realm, but since she hadn't slit his throat, she didn't consider it a problem. However, she'd never performed a manipulation of this magnitude before. Her mother had bragged constantly about her skill at shared hallucinations, how she could break down her target's identity until they weren't even sure of their own name. *But you'll get nowhere on fear alone.*

Mama had also been certain that Xan wouldn't ever be strong enough to perform one. But what Mama had thought was Xan's biggest detriment had become her most powerful advantage. Fear entwined itself with all other emotions. Fear of not being happy anymore. Fear of the good things getting ripped away. Utter, encompassing relief when a fear was resolved.

Xan had listened raptly to Mama's diatribes, but she'd never attempted to construct a shared hallucination of her own. Why change someone's entire world when she was good enough to get the job done long before it was necessary? But she'd never met a demon like Quution before. Whatever was propelling him was strong enough that she needed to change up her routine. Could she fill his mind with the thought that whatever he was planning was over? Done? His thoughts would fill in what life would be like in the aftermath and she'd be privy to it all.

She shook her head. Her first shared illusion. He wouldn't know what hit him.

~

QUUTION BLINKED HIS EYES OPEN. Xan was here. Just like he'd expected her to be.

Only her expression was nothing like he'd ever woken up to before. Her eyes were wide, her mouth hanging open as she scanned him from head to toe.

And she looked different. He couldn't quite put his finger on how. Long blond hair fanned over a purple satin pillow and rich brown irises swirled with confusion.

"What the ever-loving hell…" She shook her head and rolled to her elbow.

He frowned and glanced down at himself. Naked. Like usual. He preferred to sleep nude. But his body looked like it always had. Humanoid.

He reached his hand up to brush her cheek, but she grabbed his wrist. Inspecting his short, sharp nails, she uttered another, "What the ever-loving hell?"

Releasing him, she tufted handfuls of his hair.

He closed his eyes to enjoy her soft tugs on his scalp. Each time her fingers brushed his horns, he almost moaned. "You act like this is the first time you've woken up next to me, Xan."

Her hand stilled and she slowly drew it back. Once more, her gaze swept his body. She shook her head and adopted a flirty smile. "And how long have I woken up to you like this?"

The dam holding his always-present wave of lust back waffled and his cock stirred. "For years."

"What? Wait. You called me Xan." Her brow crinkled. "What about Brooklyn?"

He didn't use Brooklyn as a host anymore, and he didn't care for Xan being confounded. She was confident. Strong. Never bewildered like she was now.

Or pale. She seemed really pale.

She shook her head again, light hair flying in her face. Scowling, she brushed it away.

"What else would I call you?" he asked. "Are you feeling all right? You seem a little…" Wan. Anemic. Pallid. "Maybe we need to get you in the sun more."

The next look she gave him was a cross between trepidation and astonishment.

"Well, you look good. Damn good." She perused his body again, stopped at his groin, and jumped to her knees, her lush breasts swaying with the move. "So that's what you've been hiding. It's huge."

His grin was smug. He didn't need a mirror to know. "You've never complained."

Right? She hadn't, had she? For some reason, he couldn't recall their previous times together.

"No. Nope, I wouldn't have." She reached for his shaft, but he caught her wrist.

"Later. When you're feeling better."

She made to prowl closer to him, probably on top of him, but he rolled over and sat up with his back to her.

Something was off. The way she wiggled her hips should get him painfully hard, but her hips just didn't seem as wide as usual. Overall, she was less muscular. Xan was a robust female, but she seemed less so today.

"I'm feeling fine." And from the sounds of it, pissy. "What are you going to do today?"

He stretched and a sudden brush of heat ran down his spine. She was watching him. He opened his mouth to answer but no words came. What was he going to do? "I... don't know." He looked over his shoulder at her.

Her lips pursed and released. "Okay. If it was your perfect day, what would you do?"

He turned back to stare at the white wall across from his bed. White wall? That seemed off. Was the freaking wall ashen, too? Maybe the issue was him. But he couldn't look at blond-haired, doe-eyed Xan as he answered. "Make love to you all day."

She made a choking sound before she gave him the snarkiest tone possible. "We'll have to table that until I'm better." A soft sigh left her. "Are you going to...dress in your trench coat again?"

He shuddered. "Sweet brimstone, no. I'm so done with that now that the nasty business with the underworld is taken care of. I only dress when I leave the house."

He jerked his head around to the window. Ditching the bed, he went straight to the curtains and flipped them back.

Xan rushed behind him, her hand moving outside of his periphery. Was she waving?

"What do you see?" She sounded alarmed.

Grass. Trees. A lake glittering in the distance. "It's so blue."

"Yeah, it's a cloudless day?" This time, her voice rose like she was asking a question.

"No, the water." He grinned. "We should go swimming."

She put her hand on her chest, taken aback. "I don't swim."

He blinked. "You don't? Meh. You should rest anyway. I'll cook you a meal." He beelined for the door.

"Are you for fucking real?"

Stopping before he exited, he turned back. "Why?" Rolling his shoulders, he tipped his head back. His feet were planted on the floor, his body strong. His hips didn't ache, and there were no hitches in his back. All those years of being in disguise. That part was clear as a bell. He stood straight and tipped his head left and right. "If I never walk in platform boots again, it'll be too soon."

He smiled at Xan, but her brow was scrunched once again. He was dumbfounding her left and right.

She recovered and shot him a sweet smile. "Tell me again, why the getup?"

"To dupe them, remember?" Didn't she remember? Talking about his disguise tied his tongue like he was learning a foreign language.

"Oh, I remember. Tell me about it again. I love the story." She slinked back to the bed, lay across it like a Grecian goddess, and patted the satin sheets.

Sexy, but a sense of wrongness twisted in his gut. "No, you need to eat first. And no desserts for the main meal today." Maybe that's what was making her ill. He went for the door again.

"Quution, for fuck's sake, just stop."

He stopped and stared at the wood texture of the door. The more he stared, the more it resembled stone. Odd. Like so much about this morning, even the door wasn't looking quite right. He lifted his hand to touch it but…

CHAPTER 9

*X*an kept him entranced against the wall of his chamber, his sculpted ass facing her. What a magnificent backside.

He'd be happy thinking he was making her a meal. Feeding her—and probably not scavenger bugs. Or even candy beetles.

They were in the human realm—in his mind. That his fantasy was living there wasn't the surprise.

The heart-stopping shocker was his appearance. She thought she'd royally fucked up the illusion when he'd morphed into his current look, but he'd acted like *I wake up this studly every damn day*. So much about him was smaller, but Quution as a whole package seemed bigger. So much bigger.

Gone were the shanks hanging out of his mouth. He had the sexist set of fangs. She could practically see the word *ecstasy* etched into each one. Having those pierce her skin during sex would— She shivered. She would beg for it, given the chance.

And his hands. So damn humanoid, with nary a claw.

Refined. The hands of a demon scholar. Smooth hands that could pinch and plunge without drawing blood.

Her heart was still hammering at the sight of his body. She'd enchanted *him* and he'd woken up *her* ideal male. But the overall essence of him hadn't changed. He still looked like Quution, only naked. Delectably naked.

Somehow, she'd messed up her end. *You don't look well.* She could be twinsies with Brittany—Brooklyn. Did he change up and decide he liked brunettes instead?

She worried her lip with a horribly blunt tooth. How did humans consume real food? These tiny canines were no good for ripping or shredding skin. She'd have to wag her head like a dog.

And this cursed hair! She shoved the mane off her face. A dream state was an odd reality. Tangible, yet not real. She would feel everything while looking as she wished to others. It was like playing pretend and she could change her appearance with a thought.

Before he could wake, she'd changed her appearance into something she guessed he'd like. Then he'd called her Xan, like in his ideal world, he'd wake up next to her.

And her looks were confusing him and weakening the hallucination.

With a swirl of her hand, she changed her hairstyle to one with a clip. While her hallucinations weren't real, they felt real, even to her. The silky slide of the satin sheets was enough to make her consider extending her shared hallucination with Quution for an extra day and risking the wrath of Spaeth. Yes, she'd be sleeping on the same feather mattress, even if in her head, she'd feel the same comfort Quution thought he felt.

To dupe them, remember?

His trench coat and ratty pants and clunky boots were to fool…who? More importantly, why?

Spaeth, that bastard, was on to Quution, and for good reason. What was the drool-worthy demon up to?

He'd been so close to telling her. She'd get the story out of him. But she had to go find some stupid bugs so they could dine on his "home-cooked" food.

She couldn't help but sneer when she eyed the illusion over his chamber. Only they could see it, but his door was shut anyway. Yet the wood plank wasn't the "door" he was standing in front of. When he'd gone to the "window," he'd stood in front of the door. Right now, he faced a stone wall.

A human house. Not even a vampire place. What did Quution think he could do? Live as himself in the human realm, carry a briefcase, and comb over his horns before going to a nine-to-five white-collar job?

She wouldn't forget his glossy hair gliding through her fingers anytime soon. Her kind had a thing for lustrous hair. Or just she did. On Quution.

In his dream, his horns were hidden well enough that he could slap a cap on and dress in jeans and a Henley and blend. How in the underworld did he think he could just take up residence on Earth? He'd have to bond with a being from that realm.

She licked her tongue along a fang. He didn't need to be bonding with anybody.

As for her image, she concentrated on Quution. What her targets most wanted was often their greatest weakness. Quution had wanted companionship, a trusted someone to talk to, and—with a gasp, she lost all sensation of irritating hair. She was back to herself.

She peered at her hands. Were her powers failing? Mama had said maintaining these illusions were taxing, and yes, her body ached like she'd gotten into a short-lived fight, but her power stores were full. Learning to read and write hadn't taxed her innate abilities at all. Just her patience.

83

The only other explanation was that he wanted her. A lot.

~

QUUTION POLISHED off the last mouthful. He waited for Xan's reaction to the seared steak.

She chewed and gave him a guarded look from under her dark lashes.

He put his fork and steak knife on the plate. "You must've needed a good meal. You're looking better all ready."

Truthfully, she'd been back to her stunning self as soon as he'd returned to treat her to breakfast in bed. The deep purple of her skin shimmered as softly as the expensive sheets, and the light purple lines tracing her skin matched the shade of the fabric. It was like the bedding had been made for her.

"Back to normal," she said lightly.

"While I was cooking, I decided I needed a week off. You and I need to spend more time together. And you wanted to learn to read all those scrolls I was hoarding."

Her mouth curved in a pleased smile. "Excellent. And don't forget, I asked to hear the story again."

"Oh yes." He stretched and cracked his knuckles. Tensing briefly, he waited for the familiar jabs of pain, but they didn't come. He frowned at his hands. Why had he expected pain just for putting his hands together?

Xan was back to normal, but he was not.

The story snowballed, pushing at his lips to get out. He wanted to spill it so badly. "I got the idea from my sire."

"Your...sire?"

"It didn't turn out so well, but I think he had a good idea. He was selfish and self-motivated, of course. That's why it didn't work." Quution clenched his jaw. "That, and because he was an evil bastard. What he did to Stryke and our mother was unforgiveable."

She scrutinized him like she was working out a puzzle. Understanding lit her face and she sat back. "I'll be damned." She gave her head a shake. "He wasn't as clever or careful as you."

He detected a hint of humor in her tone, but his answer was serious. "No. He was driven by his need for control and domination, and his bitterness over the level of his birth ruined him. He'd positioned himself in a prime spot to make a real impact in the underworld, but he squandered it."

"How again? I don't remember."

"When my mother birthed Stryke, our sire hid them away, imprisoned them so no one could question how it was possible for two pure demons to have a halfling. But then Stryke aged and became useful to him."

"So his sire made him one of his personal servants." Xan popped the last bite of steak in her mouth. The following crunch made him tilt his head. Had he charred a portion? Her eyes flared and she chewed slowly. "Back to you."

As long as his faulty food prep didn't bother her. "Before he was killed, he came for my mother. She survived and kept me a secret."

"She loved you."

He threw his head back and laughed. "No. She was crueler than my sire. Horrendous. It's why I buried myself in books, hoping she'd forget I was there."

"Didn't she teach you to read?"

He shook his head. "During her lucid moments, she gave me a start. The books had some residual energy from the writers." Most of the ink used was blood. "I learned the rest on my own."

She arched a delicate brow. "Mm."

That sound she made. Loaded. Full of opinion she didn't want or care to voice. But he wanted to hear it.

"What was the first thing you did when you were free?" she asked.

"Go after my brother."

"You don't sound like that was a good thing." She slapped her fork down. "No way. To kill him?" Her dark eyes danced. No wonder he enjoyed telling her this story. "But you didn't, obviously. What happened?"

"Stryke's my only family." And a good guy. "We have an agreement. He pretends to work for me while being a liaison to the vampires."

"Liaison for what?"

Quution waved his hand, suddenly wary of the subject. "You know. That messy business is over with."

Her mouth tightened. "But it's part of the story. You know how much I like when you tell the whole sordid affair."

"No, I don't." He'd said it automatically. But the truth ringing in his words was undeniable. He couldn't recall telling her how his machinations had turned out. Wouldn't she have been there for them anyway?

He watched her. The area around her grew fuzzy. Blinking, he squeezed the bridge of his nose. "I…think I need to lie down."

"Now *that* I like more than talking." She rose and he got an eyeful of her body. Plump, rounded breasts, toned stomach sloping into the curves of her hips and down to the cradle of her sex. Her coloring darkened along her center, like she was draped in shadows.

She came around the table and held her hand out. He gulped and accepted it. His heart rate kicked up and he was stricken with nerves, as if he had performance anxiety.

Pulling him toward the bed, he struggled to recall when he'd put a table and chairs in his bedroom, but when he

86

looked back, they were gone. Was he drowning in lust so badly he'd blanked on the walk to his bedroom?

At the edge of the bed, she tugged him close. Face-to-face like they were, it was hard to breathe. Brimstone-laced lavender was his favorite smell and he was cocooned in it. She brushed one hand around his neck and draped one over his shoulder.

He was lost in her bottomless gaze. This close, he could see he'd been wrong. Her irises were like purple sapphires. Dark, but not as black as he'd first thought.

His gaze dropped to her full lips. Purple tinted with pink, her lips were like her eyes. She could bottle the color and make millions off the newest shade of lipstick.

She pulled him closer, and he gladly went until his mouth rested against hers. Slow. Careful. He wanted to savor his first kiss, but at the same time, he feared ruining this experience for her.

She jerked away, but didn't release him. "Haven't you ever…" Gazing deep into his eyes, she muttered, "I can't believe it."

First kiss? Surely they'd been physical before. He'd woken up to her. More than once, that he was sure of. But he was also sure he'd never lain with anyone before.

"It was the disguise," he confessed. Clarity returned, at least regarding his virtue. "I couldn't risk discovery of my half-breed status. I wouldn't pass for a full-blood like this."

"Not with that physique." She didn't make a move to kiss him again.

"Did I ruin the moment?" How had he ruined the mood? Was he so inexperienced she could tell from his lips touching hers?

He was rewarded with a small smile. This time he took control and lowered his head to capture her fuchsia lips. Licking his tongue out, he wrapped his arms around her.

Despite their seasoned steak, she tasted sweet, like the candy beetles she favored.

She was his dessert.

She met his tongue with hers and he was lost to sensation. He hardened, his erection clamped between his body and her abdomen. Hugging her closer, he deepened the kiss. Did she like it when he stroked her tongue like he wanted to stroke her sex? Would she whimper when he nibbled along her lower lip? Would she like it if he traced her lips with his tongue?

The answer to all of his questions was yes. From her moan and the way she arched into him, he could do no wrong and not one act he'd done in his life had ever infused him with such power.

He needed to touch more of her. Sweeping his hands up her body, he savored the glide of her smooth skin. Tingling along his palms matched the faint swirls under her skin. He cupped her breasts, and like with her mouth, he tested her responses. Breaking the kiss, he needed to view her body like the work of art it was.

A lift and a small squeeze had her curving into his hands, exposing her graceful neck. He used his thumb and forefinger to tweak each nipple. Her sharp inhale was perfect.

Dipping down, he captured one dark peak in his mouth. Her sugary flavor hit his tongue. Was she sweet all over?

He was painfully hard, an inferno raging in the center of his body, but he'd never been one to be distracted by his own needs. Xan came first.

Lowering to his knees, he kissed his way down her stomach.

"Quution." She licked her lips, her expression hesitant, like she thought she should put a stop to this but didn't want to. He didn't want to either.

Sliding his hands up her legs and circling until his thumbs

were wedged between the warm skin of her thighs, he continued an upward path along her legs. When his fingers hit the fiery heat of her core, he closed his eyes and fought for control.

He would not come from touching her alone. He was a grown demon, dammit.

"You need to lie down," he said gruffly, not recognizing his own voice.

She dropped, her ass almost missing the edge of the bed. With his help, she stayed on but he held her legs. She leaned back on her hands, her gaze rapt.

His hands were still on her thighs. Slowly, he pushed them apart.

Her glistening slit parted to reveal a vision that would keep him awake and hard the rest of his life. Her sex swirled with lighter purples, touches of pink, and so much wetness that he could only think of devouring her.

"I want to taste." He couldn't help uttering his thoughts. What he wanted had to be etched across his face anyway.

"I want you to." Like the sexy vixen she was, she lifted and spread her legs farther, her slender feet on his shoulders.

His groan echoed through his chamber—his room, in his cabin. Actually, he didn't care where the fuck he was, as long as nothing bothered him.

First, he had to see if she was as soft as she looked. Rimming her labia with his finger, he trailed along her fold. A light quiver ran through her legs down to her feet.

He would grin, but he was too focused.

So, so soft.

He dipped his fingertip into her slit. His groan was louder.

So wet. Dripping and ready for him and he'd done nothing but fumble along her body. A tiny nub captured his attention.

He knew what a clit was, had even read several descriptions of how to stimulate one, but this was his first time seeing the special organ in person.

Mine.

With the lightest touch, he circled her clit. Her hips bucked and her moan went straight to his dick. He stroked down her seam until his finger skimmed her opening.

Her legs were rigid, like she was on the edge.

"Do you like this?" He needed the answer more than his next breath.

"I like it all, just do more of it," she said between clenched teeth.

His grin was quick, fading as he licked his lips. Inserting the tip of his finger, he dropped his head to flick his tongue across her nub.

"Quution! Yes," she hissed.

Thrusting his finger in the rest of the way, he marveled over how she clenched around him. He slid back out, then ran his finger up to circle her clit and back down to thrust inside.

She let out a shout and her knees fell even farther open.

Her wet sex open to him, he feasted, using his mouth to suck, lick, and nibble until she grasped each horn and pushed herself against his face. How he had the cognition to keep a thrusting rhythm with his finger, he didn't know.

He didn't care as long as her pleasure-heavy shouts and moans rang through his place. His head couldn't move, she had him pulled against her so hard. When her body tightened around him, she stilled for a brief moment before shaking with convulsions. He nearly spilled his own release.

He hadn't so much as touched himself, but lapping Xan's juice, getting slammed with her orgasm, was almost enough to get himself off.

With his help, she strung out her release and he was

happy to let her go as long as she needed. As soon as she was done, he wanted to know when he could do it again.

Finally, she released him, her arms flopping next to her, her legs going limp and sliding off his shoulders.

He rose enough to pick her up and set her down across the bed. Her desire fulfilled, heavy-lidded eyes tracked him.

He grinned. "Was that okay for my first try?"

"It was adequate." She failed to hold back her smile. Her bared fangs in his bed sent another shot of electricity through him.

What if he used his energy in bed?

No, he had to know what he was doing before he shocked his partner.

Stretching over her, he placed a knee between hers.

She stiffened and put a hand on his chest. "Wait. This will be, like, your *first time* first time?"

"Yes."

She slid her gaze away, the furrow in her brow back. "It should be special."

Was it ever for demons? He was a lottery winner right now. "This is special. *You* are special."

Instead of melting under him, her gaze shimmered with guilt. "Has a female ever gotten you off? Do you even know what it's like?"

There was no derision in her questions. She was asking out of concern, and she must've read his answer in his face.

Slipping out from under him, he was left facing the useless softness of the sheets. He'd had the most mind-shattering experience ever, but she was leaving. He must've misread her statement.

He'd only been adequate.

CHAPTER 10

*T*hat climax could've killed her. She'd ridden the wave of rapture so long she hadn't been sure where she ended and Quution's wicked, naughty mouth started.

Had he studied sexual gratification as much as he'd researched those scrolls?

She'd been so ready to fuck him. Take the broad tip of him inside and slam him in the rest of the way.

But he was a vir— She almost gagged on the word. Quution's brawny strength didn't make one think virginal thoughts. And she should lose her demon card for allowing his V card to stop her from jumping him. Why couldn't she lay with him during this deception? It wasn't like he was going to want her when he learned she was nothing but a run-of-the-mill spy. She was using him to save her family and that didn't have to include sex.

His sigh drew her attention. Her heart twisted. He looked so dejected. Waves of inadequacy rolled off him. He was afraid he'd disappointed her.

If she had a cruel streak, she'd leave him to his massive

erection. He could get himself off with a mediocre hand job, or wait for the lust to fade.

But there was her mission. If he thought he couldn't satisfy her, what good was she? He might be afraid to tell her about what he thought he'd accomplished in the underworld. What great fear had she resolved for him with this fantasy?

"Lie on your back," she ordered.

He flipped over, his gaze inquiring, and there it was. She could stare at his cock for hours. No scales. No barbs. And he definitely wouldn't spew poison with his ejaculation. Even ridged with veins, he was smooth, his ball sac heavy.

She crawled between his legs. His lips parted like he couldn't believe she still wanted anything to do with him.

"You need the full range of experience," she said. "So many of us lose out on it." In their realm, most demons' first times were stolen by bigger, stronger, more evil demons. She couldn't be just another soulless beast.

Teaching him about the possibilities of passion would be her apology. Then he could lose himself with someone who really cared about him.

Her throat tightened. *She* cared about him. But not more than the ones who relied on her for their safety.

He raised himself to his elbows. "Are you all right? You don't have to—"

Enough dark thoughts. She had the rest of the week for her mission and if she did this right, he'd be putty for her to mold. "I want to." And she really did.

She wrapped her hand around his shaft. He dropped to his back, his head hitting with a muted *thunk*. Licking the rim of his cock, she took her time. He pressed his heels into the mattress and bucked his hips.

"Sorry." His voice was taut.

"Don't be. I can take the ride." With that, she sucked him into her mouth.

His groan went on for a full ten seconds, growing stronger as she pulled more of him in. Forcing her throat to relax, she took as much of him as possible.

"Xaaaan." His breath sawed in and out of his chest, and his body shook with restraint. If her mouth weren't full, she'd tell him to just let go. This was his first time getting head and his first time with a female; she didn't expect to be on him for an hour.

But she would if she could. He tasted like a well-seasoned fillet, smoked to the perfect flavor. A treat for her normally sweet tooth.

She flicked her tongue up and down his length, tasting, savoring. Her core tingled and warmed and she would love to tutor him during another round of oral. Not that she had to teach him a thing. He'd been a master as soon as he'd started.

He crunched up, his hands clasping her scalp, then falling away like he didn't know what to do with them. "Xan. I'm going to…I'm going to…"

His cock kicked in her mouth as his orgasm hit.

His mouth dropped open to roar just as heavy pounding rattled his door. Confusion rippled over his face, freezing his shout, but not stopping his release.

She froze, her mouth still over him. No, they couldn't get interrupted. It might ruin the illusion and she hadn't had enough time to cement the hallucination. One more day and he would've told her everything.

His hot release spilled. She drank him down, but inside she was panicking.

Who was it?

More knocking. "Quution. Open up. We need to talk."

Fuck her sideways, it was Stryke.

She released Quution's shaft. He gasped and tried to sit up, but the aftereffects of his orgasm were too strong.

"What the fuck," he gasped.

Another knock, harder than the first two, made them both spin their heads around.

"Just wait!" Quution's stunned gaze met hers. He reached for her, but she scurried backward, dropping off the stone slab. Without her concentration, the illusions dissolved, ending the hallucination.

She was in so much trouble.

His expression faltered as he looked around.

Stryke heaved the door open. "Are you okay? I thought I heard…" His violet gaze landed on her. Her first coherent thought was that his eyes were the wrong color of purple; she much preferred the lighter lilac. He stopped mid motion and shoved a hand through his hair. He pivoted like he was going to turn around to give them privacy, but the stone wall was in his way.

Quution blinked and looked around. She hated herself as she watched understanding dawn on him.

"You tricked me," he said.

Stryke snapped to attention, his gaze turning accusatory. He probably thought she was fucking Quution for information. Self-hate roiled inside her. He wouldn't be wrong.

"Why, Xan?" Quution slung the question like a whip. "Who are you working for?"

Energy crackled through the room. She had to get out of here, but Stryke blocked the only exit. Two energy demons had her trapped.

She left the only way she knew how. Squeezing her eyes shut, she concentrated.

The next time she opened them, she was in Marcus and had to jerk the wheel to avoid a moving van. Good, he wasn't at home. Quution knew where Marcus lived, but he didn't know what the human drove.

~

"Xan!" Quution roared. He pulled the blanket over himself, but he needn't have bothered. He was back in grungy clothing, sprawled on his hard slab, and looking for the female of his literal dreams. His dick was hanging outside his pants, though. Rearranging himself with shaking hands, he tried to find an excuse for this situation, anything but the truth.

Had they really been intimate with each other, or was it all in his imagination? It had felt real. His cock was still wet from her mouth. Or was it his seed? He didn't know up from down at the moment.

Stryke clenched his fists and looked around. "She's the spy Melody warned me about."

Xan. A spy. He'd known that, but when had he fooled himself into thinking she was hanging around because she liked him?

"How would Melody know?" Forming a complete sentence was a struggle. Xan was gone. They'd been—they were just having—she'd just… He couldn't think in a complete sentence.

"There's talk the full-bloods don't trust you, but she doesn't know who's spearheading it. I came to ask if anyone's been lurking."

Xan didn't lurk. "They've never trusted me." They just hadn't been devious about it before. "I can find her. I know where her host lives." He growled and flung off his sheet. He'd have to possess his host first, then go looking for Marcus.

"You find a host. I'll follow Xan's trail." Stryke shimmered, about to disappear.

"No."

Stryke's form solidified and he scowled. "Why the hell not?"

"I need to talk to her."

Stryke narrowed his eyes, his gaze taking in the rumpled bedding. "Perhaps you aren't the one who should be interrogating her."

"Don't hurt her," Quution said between clenched teeth. "Detain her. I'm the one she fooled." He'd been so careful about his ruse, but he'd been so easily duped by a warm and willing body.

What kind of power did she have? She pounced on weaknesses, he'd figured out that much about her. He'd just never thought she'd use it on him, not to that level.

Stryke disappeared, and Quution paced his room. He couldn't leave. If Stryke found Xan and she popped out of Marcus, she'd come right back to where she'd left.

His energy pumped as he secured all of his wards. She might be able to saunter in, but he'd make sure she wouldn't be able to leave until he had his answers.

XAN MANEUVERED into a grocery store parking lot. Her hands were shaking, her angst affecting her host. Good thing he had a strong heart.

She parked and killed the engine. A perfectly good day she could've spent in an imaginary bed seeking sexual gratification over and over again had taken a turn for the *oh shit what should I do now?*

Rubbing her hands on her scalp, she tried to think of her next move. Where should she go? How long could she stay in Marcus in one shot? When would Quution leave his room so she could return and find her sister? Because Spaeth wasn't going to take this news well.

She had to think, to plan, but her mind kept returning to the shattered look in Quution's eyes when he realized she'd been playing him. Slamming the steering wheel, she let out a bark of frustration. The horn blared and she grimaced.

Brimstone filled the interior and she tensed. Crackling energy brushed over her skin. The sensation didn't pool in her belly and make her dream of twisted sheets and sunset horns, though.

It wasn't Quution.

She glared at the demon in the passenger seat. Why'd she have to fuck with an energy demon, and why'd he have to have a brother? One that gave a shit about him on top of it. Energy demons' powers were the envy of the underworld. They could bend all kinds of rules the rest of them had to follow.

Like following her energy to her host. Instead of panicking that Stryke had found her, her first emotion was disappointment that it wasn't Quution.

Violet eyes glared back at her. His horns were hidden in his hair, and at some point, he'd figured out how to travel between realms while keeping his clothes on. She didn't bother getting out of the car to run. It'd draw attention and the police were a giant nuisance for a possessed human. And Stryke would be able to find her anywhere.

"Why are you spying on Quution?" he growled. The voice wasn't the one she wanted to hear either.

No wonder Quution kept up the disguise. If he ditched the fangs and brushed his hair back, everyone would know he and Stryke were full brothers.

She could take that information to Spaeth, but that wouldn't be enough. Besides, her shaky sense of honor made her loath to reveal Quution's past. The bargain they'd made should be ironclad. He'd taught her to read and she wanted—needed—to hold up her end.

"Tell me," Stryke bit out.

She rolled her eyes toward him. "My business with your brother is none of yours."

"Not how it works." He slapped his hand on Marcus's bulky shoulder and energy buzzed through her.

The contact was enough for her muted powers to travel through her host to Stryke. She couldn't dig into him as if they were in the underworld, but she got the impression of a female and the type of fear that always accompanied love— the fear of losing it.

"Shouldn't you make sure your mate's okay?" she asked sweetly.

Stryke bared his teeth, but a moment of indecision passed through his eyes. Yes, she'd sensed it. His mate was sick—no, not sick. She had a condition, a well-handled one, but he worried about her.

Xan sent out her energy, feeding his fear that his mate had sickened while he was gone.

His gaze flickered with terror, but his mouth tightened.

She upped her game and wove in his mate crying out his name. His whole body vibrated as his eyes narrowed. He snapped up Marcus's phone in the console and punched in a number.

A female answered.

"Doing okay, babe?" Stryke asked.

"Yeah. Whose phone is this?"

"A demon's host. The one who's hustling Q."

Xan arched a brow. Presumptuous ass.

Stryke glared at her. "She was messing with me. Tell ya later." He disconnected and tossed the phone back down. "Well, who are you working for?"

"Why can't I like Quution for who he is?"

"Because you're a demon."

"So are you."

"I'm different." He was completely serious. Ass.

"Offense taken."

"I don't care."

She would like Stryke if he weren't blocking her sister's ticket out of captivity. Her powers might be metaphysically constrained inside of Marcus, but she had centuries of experience. Unlike Mama, Xan had realized cunning and experience could compensate for a limited range of powers.

Stryke and Quution were brothers and they worked together. Stryke had to care about Quution and vice versa. What were typical fears for a loved one? That answer hit close to home.

Xan lived under the constant stress each day that Xera suffered pain and torture. That she would die and Xan would be helpless to stop it.

"I know you're worried about Quution," she said. A muscle jumped in Stryke's jaw. She was on to something, but it was too broad. "You should be. They're on to him."

"Who's they?"

Good question. She could allude to the danger without confirming who was behind it. "Isn't it always the others on the Circle?"

Stryke's eyes narrowed, and he glanced out the windshield. "I already know that. But who?"

So he knew. Quution knew. But then, they thought she was spying on Quution and she was on the Circle. "I don't think you have to worry about that. I think you should be more concerned with just how upset they'll be when they find out what you and Quution are up to. And your vampire friends."

An eye twitch. She was narrowing it down.

Stryke faced her, his stony expression setting her progress back to zero. "You act like you care about him, but you're either investigating him for your own purposes, or because you're a half-breed working for someone else."

It was all she could do not to wince. "I care about him." Unfortunately, that was true.

"Then if you don't want to see him decapitated, dismembered, or otherwise mutilated, then you need to stay away from him."

Not an option. And Quution was powerful. No being in the underworld was untouchable, but taking him down would require more than one demon, more than two. The demons would have to unify. What reason would be so great that he'd inspire unheard of levels of hate in their realm?

The way he'd looked out of the cabin in the woods that didn't exist crossed through her mind. He seemed awfully protective of the human realm. Less so of the underworld. He didn't associate with others unless he had business with another member of the Circle.

It was like he wanted to live up here. But demons could still get at him.

What if they couldn't?

What was he up to?

"What he's planning will get him killed no matter what realm he hides in," she said. Her ability in a host was muted, but it was logical to assume Stryke feared for his brother's safety.

"Not if they can't get to him." Stryke's lips pressed together like he'd said too much.

She slid her gaze away, not wanting to let him know that she was thinking hard on what he said. His feelings on the subject swelled to near terror levels, but no one would be able to tell just by looking at him. Cool. But she could.

Body language was as telling as feelings, as long as she knew what to look for. A little curl of his fingers, wanting to make fists. A jaw that could carve marble. Shoulders so tight they'd started to quiver.

Such a telling statement. *Not if they can't get to him*. Stryke could come and go at will. The Circle member that used to be human, Melody, could as well. The rest of them needed to recruit humans, form cults of devoted followers who could be enticed into reciting the proper incantation to allow their bodies to be used as hosts. It was a tedious process that was nearly impossible if one didn't know the right people. She planned to hang on to Marcus until he took his last breath, even if it meant tolerating his obnoxious self-loathing for having acquiesced to his cult-loving ex-girlfriend.

What was Quution up to? Was he plotting a way to close them off from this plane of existence? Demons sure as hell couldn't get to him then.

Betrayal snaked through her. Quution was devising a way to tether her people to the underworld, robbing them of their small windows of freedom from the travesties that regularly occurred in their own realm.

It's so blue.

He loved this realm. His fantasy was being here, living in some remote cabin, and cooking for the love of his life.

"Do you want to see that happen to him, Xan?" Stryke asked. "Or do you want to make sure it doesn't happen? Which one is it?"

She swallowed the bile that crept up her throat.

Stryke was watching her, waiting for answers, like she was just going to spill her woes to a random demon because he thought he'd cornered her in a car. He was arrogant, just like his brother.

The corner of her mouth lifted in a snarl. She concentrated. As she left Marcus's body to return to Quution's chamber, she grinned at Stryke's enraged shout.

CHAPTER 11

*X*an's bare feet hit the gritty floor of Quution's chamber. He was there, his massive back toward her, his hands clasped behind his back. Blood droplets trailed down his wrists. Had he scraped himself with his ridiculous claws? Probably.

He spun around. Fury, hurt, and relief passed through his features.

Seeing him now, she didn't notice the costume, seeing beyond it to the real him instead. His shoulders were just as broad, though he'd adopted the hitch. That's right, the shoes.

She stalked toward him. He didn't move but his gaze was wary. When she reached him, she pulled her arm back like a lever and slapped him across the face.

He blinked and touched his cheek with his fingers. The air crackled, but it wasn't his energy. Stryke had arrived.

Air buzzed around her and she couldn't move. One of them had immobilized her.

"You're going to imprison us down here." She wanted to slap him again, for so many reasons. And she was furious at herself for it. A slap? That was so…emotional. She should've dug into his skin with her claws, attacked his jugular with her fangs, and tried to rip his lying head from his body. At least that would have accomplished something.

Except he'd never lied. His deep, dark secrets would curse her and Xera forever. And her poor niece, of course. It wouldn't matter if Xan begged Quution and Stryke to help her save her sister, they would be stuck here, at the mercy of Spaeth and any other full-blood and half-breed who could overpower them.

Might made right in the underworld. And most demons didn't know what mercy was.

Quution lifted his gaze over her shoulder.

She didn't wait for Stryke to answer the unspoken question. "No, he didn't tell me. I figured it out. I might not be able to read all of your precious books, but I still have a brain." She wanted to point an accusing finger at Stryke, but only her mouth could move. At least she could glare at Quution while she spoke. "He's scared for you. I had to wonder why. You're not the type to take over. For all of us halfings, you're like the symbol of hope that not every full-blood is a demented monster. And your powers are the gold standard of the realm."

Blood drained from Quution's face and his gaze darted to Stryke once again. His brother being in on the plan was a given, but how high up did it go? It certainly didn't have roots in the underworld beyond Quution. So the vampires? Had Quution's mission been sanctioned by the vampire government?

Betrayal burned through her. The brothers had trapped her like she was the villain.

"You're not the type to take over. You work from the shadows," she continued. "You're devious, underhanded. You don't get your fake claws dirty. So I had to ask myself, why would a powerful demon pretend to be something he's not?

What would he be up to? He's protective of humans and has connections with the vampires." She cocked her head. "And his fantasy takes place on Earth, in the great wide open, the very opposite of how he was raised. It was pretty clear after that."

Tendrils of guilt floated through his features. "And if you're right, who would you take this information to?"

"Everyone," she lied. Could she do that to him? Taking her theory to Spaeth would free Xera, but at what cost? Spaeth would easily rally his fellow full-bloods and be able to recruit most every other half-breed.

The option to escape to the human realm had always been the halflings only respite. Hours of peace. Even if they were in a host to do another demon's bidding, they were still allowed time to themselves, where they could watch TV, eat all varieties of food, and learn new skills like driving.

Quution was going to take that away from all of them.

Stryke's boots crunched as he circled around her to stand by Quution. He crossed his arms. Nope, he wasn't as good-looking as Quution. "Do you realize how it'd destabilize the realm if you spread those lies?"

The blame was not on her. She would be going from one service contract with Spaeth to an eternity with whomever could catch her or blackmail her. "We all know they're not lies. I'm sure more of your vampire friends know it as well."

She would tap her foot, but her limbs remained immobile.

Quution dared step closer. She couldn't move, but she could spit. It wouldn't burn like Spaeth's but it might give her a smidgeon of satisfaction.

"Xan." His voice was soft. "Tell us who's making you do this."

"I work alone. Always."

He took another step toward her, reading her like one of

his books. "Yes. I've realized that. But not this time. You won the prize for most unexpected demon to take a Circle position but since then, you've remained isolated. Except for me. Unlike the rest of us, you have no one working for you, no servants. I'd like to think you're actually interested in forming a stable government, but you haven't even attended any meetings."

"I have too."

"Late enough to have missed the whole thing. Why have you done all this?" He cocked his head. "And for whom?"

Damn him. He sounded like he actually cared. She lifted her chin. "You tell me everything first."

"It was my idea," Quution said. Stryke shot him a hard look, but Quution continued. "Like you said, I care for the beings in the other realm. I can't say the same for the majority of species down here. We both know if I set wards against full-bloods only, there are plenty of other half-breeds who are just as cruel."

His idea. He'd thought of it. He'd planned it. And he'd be the one carrying it out. All those hours studying their kind's history, reading every tome and scroll he could find. And he said it was the others who were cruel.

"Now, it's your turn," Quution said, his calm so aggravating. "Who do you report to? A full-breed, one on the Circle?"

"I didn't say I'd talk if you did."

Stryke snorted. "Then I guess you're going to stay here until you do."

Quution jerked his gaze to his brother. "Not here. Her master will know she's here."

She almost spit at the word master, but it was heartbreakingly accurate. Her heart hit her ribs. She willed it to slow down. The next time Spaeth summoned her and she didn't show, Xera would pay.

She had the rest of the week. Wherever they kept her, she had six more days to try to escape.

"No," Quution said. "Absolutely not." Stryke's idea was ludicrous, and it made him nauseous. "I wouldn't put my worst enemy in there."

"She *is* your worst enemy." Stryke's tone was as flat as his stare.

No, she wasn't. Unfortunately, Quution had no proof. Xan had been the only demon to get close enough to hurt him and she'd done it without drawing blood. Her kind were rumored to be empaths, but he'd never pondered the meaning of the designation. Xan dealt only in fear, but from what he'd witnessed, she was adept at all the nuances that went along with the emotion. She preyed on weakness, and there were so many things that could make a being weak, if only for a moment.

She didn't just make a guy think spiders were all over the floor, she did what she said. She warped their perception of that fear, either making her target go out of their mind with panic or deliriously happy when she made them believe their fear was resolved.

The way she could pinpoint what he wanted most—he hadn't even known himself how much he feared he would never reach a state of peace, of utter bliss. Like he'd felt with her. Not once during their day together had he looked over his shoulder. His thoughts hadn't been consumed with strategy, or spells bouncing around in his brain, or debilitating what-ifs. He'd just enjoyed his time with her. And it'd all been fake.

The devastation when it had all vanished after a knock at the door… His chest still hurt.

And if the very real hurt her con had inflicted wasn't bad enough, her taste was still on his lips. Her cries still rang in his ears and he recalled exactly what she felt like in his arms.

How had that been fake?

A very tangible Xan was in his chamber while he and Stryke conversed outside his door. Between the two of them, she wasn't going anywhere.

What she had done was despicable. To do it, she must lack empathy, sympathy, and compassion—she was a true demon.

Yet he could not make himself imprison her in the cell he'd been raised in.

"There are plenty of areas we can keep her." The underworld was a labyrinth, a realm that had never been fully mapped.

"But are they set up to keep a person inside?"

"One of us is going to have to be with her constantly anyway." *He* would be with her constantly.

"Between us and Melody, we can keep her contained."

Quution shook his head. "No, not Melody. The less she knows, the better." Xan wasn't the only spy in the underworld, and because of her association with him, Melody was already under scrutiny.

Stryke studied him for a heartbeat. Quution bristled and met his gaze. Energy crackled between them.

"I don't trust you around her," Stryke said. "She's gotten to you. I mean, you two were…"

"I know full well what we were doing," Quution said tightly. No reminders necessary. It was heartless how she'd toyed with him, but he couldn't bring himself to regret one second.

Until he recalled how she hadn't wanted to have sex with him.

Quution tired of the argument. Xan would pester Stryke

until there was an altercation and one of them got hurt. Either outcome was unacceptable. "I'm close to figuring out how to bind our kind down here while allowing those who have mates on Earth free access." Otherwise, Stryke and Melody would be trapped in the underworld for eternity while their mates were in the other realm. "I'd be studying anyway."

"Fine, but I'm stopping by to check on you. Frequently. We just need to figure out where."

"My library. She's the only one who's been able to find it."

Stryke dragged in a breath and held it like he was trying not to sigh. "And just who has she told?"

"I've sensed no others trying to enter."

The almost imperceptible shake of Stryke's head aggravated Quution. Since Stryke had arrived, he'd been relegated to the role of little brother, and it chafed.

Stryke opened his mouth, but Quution interrupted. "I'm not asking permission."

"I'm passing along what's going on down here."

Quution tipped his head. Notifying Demetrius, who could bring the situation to his government, was smart. If the problem of a certain sexy purple demon snowballed out of his control, it was best others knew the situation.

"I'm close to sealing the underworld." Quution just had to figure out how to make his wards all-encompassing so he could seal them up as he left the realm forever. Demons were worse than lawyers about exploiting loopholes. The spells couldn't be layered arbitrarily.

"I guess all that's left here is to see if she's going to walk or if we have to carry her."

Quution looked at his door, wishing he could see through to the immobilized demon behind it.

He wasn't sure he liked either of Stryke's options.

CHAPTER 12

Three more days before Xan had to report to Spaeth. Stress should be gnawing at her. Spaeth would demand answers. She needed information to free her sister and niece, though if she were honest, she doubted Spaeth's word. He'd find a way to exploit her some more, but all Xan needed was to know where he was holding her family.

Three days. She didn't know if she'd survive the boredom.

With nothing to do the last two days, she'd recited the alphabet, spelled out her thoughts for the practice, sung songs, whatever it took to pass the time. Quution's back was to her, and energy wards halved the dusty library. She'd slept on the floor—right next to the line of energy preventing her from crossing to him. The buzz of Quution's energy over her skin had nothing to do with her reasoning.

Each time she crept closer to his wards, his shoulders tightened. He was aware of her. Painfully.

If the line of demarcation weren't also imbued with Stryke's energy, she could've strolled across it and sat in Quution's lap.

She'd been here long enough to study the barrier in detail. She could get through it, but Quution hadn't left the library. Once a day, the demon brothers would take her to a cave with a pool of water that amazingly didn't smell like a brackish lagoon. Taking a pleasant dip with Quution wasn't an option, but she lingered as long as their patience allowed, then pushed it even further. She liked the way Quution started pacing and clearing his throat and Stryke's furtive glances toward him. He was worried about Quution's feelings for her.

Currently, she perched on the little desk she used to read on. He'd taken away many of the other pieces of furniture on her side of the barrier and cleared off the shelves. When she'd asked for a book to read, he'd asked, "Who are you reporting to?"

The last two days had provided her with copious amounts of time to think about Xera. Had Xera been exposed to Spaeth enough to detect his weakness and capitalize on it yet? Perhaps her niece's powers were developing and she could see a missing layer Xera hadn't yet.

Either way, they'd been Spaeth's prisoners for months and Xan was beginning to think she'd failed Xera. A good two hundred and twenty years older than Xera, Xan had ignored Mama's taunts that Xera was the powerful daughter she'd always wanted. Instead, she had taken her role as older sister seriously and passed on all the secrets of their purple kind.

The first rule: the longer she was exposed to a target, the higher the chance of success. Spaeth could stick Xera in a hole in the wall and chant every spell in the book, but after all this time, Xera should've been able to divine a way out.

Xan was caught between debilitating anxiety that Spaeth was hurting the females every chance he got and ignorant hopefulness that Xera had escaped with Xoda and Spaeth was bluffing.

She believed in Xera's power. Their mama had done what she could to mold Xera's thinking to her own bloody doctrine, citing Xan as the failure that shouldn't have been allowed to survive. But Xan had refused to let Xera think she was nothing but a pawn for Mama to use. And when Mama had been ready to farm Xera out to the highest bidder, Xan had put a stop to it. Permanently. Then she'd taken over Xera's training.

Mama had assumed Xan wasn't strong enough to best her. It was why Xan had been shoved out of the nest. *You ask too many questions. Your powers are stunted. You're useless. Useless.* Deep down, she'd known it was because she'd resisted Mama's efforts to manipulate her. Mama had probably found a second demon to procreate with just to birth another child she could use.

Xan's mind churned through scenarios until she could combust from insanity.

"Brimstone and ashes, Quution, can I just get one fucking book?" A little more tact might be required, but he should know by now that she wasn't spilling her guts to him. So why make her suffer?

"Who are you reporting to?"

So that was how he was going to play it. She made a request—albeit a bitchy one—and he returned with the same old question.

"I guess I'll just chat then." After two days stuck in her own mind with a sexy, frustrating demon only feet away, she could converse with the wind. "Stryke, huh? Did he know about you? You know, I had a sister I didn't know about."

Xan pressed her lips together. She hadn't meant to go there. But she could talk about Xera. Quution wouldn't make the connection. He'd just assume her sister was like her and off doing spy stuff.

Besides, it got Quution to turn his head. He might even be able to see her out of the corner of his eye.

"Mama was a… She was ambitious. Like demon-y ambitious. When it was clear I was incompatible with her outlook on life"—like refusing to allow Mama to sell her by the hour —"she kicked me out and had another kid. Thankfully, it took a while for her to conceive again."

Quution had gone back to staring at the scroll in front of him, but his shoulders weren't as tense as before. He was thinking about what she'd said.

"I should've seen it coming." Xan lost herself to those days. Of turning around and spotting eyes the color of an aged merlot. "Mama sent my little sister to spy on me. Jealousy, I suspect. It gets a lot of my kind. We only have female babies, you know."

He turned his head again. The rich orange of his horns peeked out above his hairline. No, he hadn't known.

"There's like this rivalry built into my breed of demon," she explained. "It's why you don't see many of us." That, and other demons killed them on sight before they could become victims. "Only female births, and then the constant fear of being used by our kin. It makes them trigger-happy."

"Them?"

She would've grinned, but he'd taken her by surprise. A question that wasn't *Who do you report to?* But as for clarifying what he'd asked, her words caught in her throat.

She'd just wanted a family. A home. Someone to watch her back while she did the same for them.

"I… I'm not as bloodthirsty, I guess. I don't know who my sire was, but I assume I get it from him. Mama killed her mama. Mama had no sisters—she'd killed any that survived. I saw the idiocy of the trend." Her laugh lacked all humor. "I didn't miss the irony when I had to kill Mama."

His chair squeaked as he swiveled around. "You killed your own mother?"

If his tone had been full of censure, she might have shut down the conversation and gone back to mind-numbing boredom. "It was necessary."

"The sister you didn't know about."

"Mm." She didn't dare delve into the circumstances behind the fatal fight with Mama. Quution was smart enough to put together that if she'd kill to protect her sister, she was probably protecting her sister now. "I have a niece, too."

"There are *three* of you?"

"Oh, they're not like me." The statement rolled out so fast, Xan blinked. Sure, Xera could be a cold-hearted bitch, but that was part of Underworld Survival 101. "Xera's half-breed sire—did I say Xera? I meant Xoda. Her sire had more brawn than brains, I guess, from what Xera said. We joke that Xoda will only be able to give people the dream about going to work with no pants on." She smiled at the beat of relief that went through her. She always enjoyed talking about her niece, and she'd missed it. Without Xera around, there was no Xoda.

A smile touched Quution's lips, but his gaze was introspective. "Xoda—sister or niece?"

"Niece. Xera is my sister."

"Does Xera manipulate fear?"

Xan crossed her legs where she sat on top of her desk. This was a distinction she had to make. "We can manipulate all emotions. Some of my kind"—all the rest—"can sense them all and bend them to their will. Not telepathy, exactly. We can't read minds. Or speak into them. But we can influence emotions. My specialty is fear."

There. She'd answered without confirming that Xera could warp happiness, worry, anger…anything.

His expression hardened. "And that thing with me?"

"That thing with you came from your imagination. I created something like a dream state from the fantasy in your mind. We all dream of what life would be like if 'insert fear here' weren't an issue."

"But you were in it."

She cocked a brow. "I tried looking like that host you used and you claimed I was pale and must be ill, remember?"

His scowl was laughable. "How did I cook for you?"

"Weaknesses are malleable. You feared I wouldn't eat, so I fed your imagination that you were cooking for me."

"But we ate. It was a steak."

"That hunk of steak was candy beetles." She shook her head. He wasn't getting it. "The more tangible a hallucination, the better. When a fear demon starts manipulating a dream, the target thinks the fear is being resolved, and their mind gets euphoric and feeds the manipulator the information she needs. It's pure relief for you, thus giving me more power and making the outcome more believable."

His jaw dropped, but in his eyes he was horrified. "That's an astonishing power."

Her back went ramrod straight. "And wielding energy so it can imprison me with nothing more than a thought isn't?"

"It wasn't a criticism. There are so many layers to what you're capable of, it's mind-boggling."

She did a little wiggle that was a lot like preening. No one had complimented her powers. Ever. She was too much of a halfling to her own kind, and too threatening to the rest of demonkind—and avoided at all costs. "Not all of us can induce a hallucination." She wasn't a boaster—usually. Today, apparently she was. "Nor can we all hold them for long periods of time." *Like I did with you.*

Maybe his own energy had added fuel to her flame? Could that even happen? It wasn't like they were mates or anything.

"So you're powerful." He said it so simply, like it confirmed what he'd been thinking.

"I've worked hard to hone my abilities." Her sister was powerful. That Spaeth had bested her…

He leaned forward in his chair, his elbows on his legs. "You could've kept me imprisoned in my chamber with nothing but a thought."

She swept her hand from one end of the room to the other, indicating the energy shield. "Isn't that what you're doing?"

He straightened abruptly like she'd affronted him. Then his brows dropped. "Most of our powers have a significant mental component, I guess."

"Why do you want to make it so we can't ever visit the human realm?"

His lilac eyes shuttered. "What do demons usually do when they're up there?"

"They don't wreak as much havoc as you think."

"Why are you in Marcus?" Arrogance stained his speech. "It's to work for your full-blooded master."

Her indignant gasp echoed through the library chamber. Marcus had nothing to do with Spaeth. "I guess you don't know as much as you think you do."

While his brow dropped as he contemplated what she meant, she slid off the desktop and stomped to the corner she'd been sleeping in.

He thought she was nothing more than an unthinking minion. Fine. He could do all the thinking without her. And when he fell asleep, she'd traipse through his wards and leave.

≈

WHY'D SHE QUIT TALKING? She'd never quit bugging him before. Must be sensitive about the master comment. The half-breeds on the Circle were overwhelmingly smug about their status and had formed a posse of their own, minus Xan.

She had to be working with someone. She didn't have servants of her own, unless it was the mysterious sister and niece she'd suddenly mentioned. Had Xan and her sister come up with the idea of spying on him? But if so, what was their ultimate aim?

He was more confused about Xan than before and he hated having her back to him. It was too early to bed down for the night and he dreaded another round on the hard dirt floor.

She could conjure the illusion of another plush mattress with satin sheets for them.

He spun his chair around, the squeak bouncing through the chamber. After who knew how many minutes had passed with him staring blankly at the scroll, he spun back around.

Her shapely ass faced him. The slope of her hips down to her waist was a sight worth painting and hanging on his wall. Torchlight gleamed along her smooth scalp. The image of her sucking on him rose so swiftly he slammed back in the rickety chair.

He wanted to touch her again. Feel her come against his mouth, his hand, and—

He shoved both hands through his hair and growled when two of his fake claws stabbed him, one in the cheek and one above his right eye.

Fuck, he hated this costume. It hurt.

Throughout his duress, she didn't twitch.

He'd really upset her. Why did he care?

It was time for lunch. No, she'd eaten scavenger bugs and

he'd had a submarine sandwich Stryke had brought down. His brother was becoming most proficient at bringing items into the underworld. It was beneficial since Quution couldn't leave, and he couldn't stomach bugs or beetles.

Though he must've done fine a few days ago when she'd tricked him into eating candy beetles.

No wonder she'd tasted so sweet.

"It's time for dinner," he said gruffly. "Want to split the remains of my sandwich?"

A scratching noise emanated from the wall by her. A line of beetles swarmed toward her head. She must be using her ability to make them flee an imaginary enemy. One fat bug skittered straight for her. She snatched it and the audible crunch gave him his answer.

She needed time. He hadn't anticipated that she'd want to chitchat, since he'd locked her in this room and wouldn't even give her a book. But he had liked her attempts to talk with him.

In reality, no one conversed with him in this realm. Demons spoke with him out of necessity, or when they were trying to kill him, not for conversation.

Pulling his sandwich out of the blue and white cooler, he savored the sounds of her crunching. It'd been less than ten minutes since she'd quit talking to him and he was as empty as a water bottle in the Sahara.

Chewing through his sandwich, he tasted nothing beyond a generic chalk flavor. Earlier, the food had been good. Xan had rejected sharing it then, too, but it hadn't hit him as hard then.

His gaze landed on the stack of books he'd cleared from her half of the library. The entire stack wasn't entirely demonic ramblings; there were a few good reads in the pile. One nightmare demon had been especially eloquent and had penned all the dreams of his human hosts. Quution had found it quite entertaining, and given Xan's level of proficiency, she could probably read the whole thing with little trouble.

He finished his sandwich and crinkled the wrapping in his hand. As he crossed his half of the library, he wedged the bundle onto the torch. The blast of burning paper dwindled to the normal brimstone scent of the realm.

No more scavenger beetles propelled out of the walls. Xan must be done eating. He went to the seam his energy wards made in the middle of the room and set the book on the floor. Without a word, he pushed it through.

She glanced over her shoulder, but not at him. Her gaze touched on the book before she turned back to the wall. Disappointment rang through him.

Given what he'd done to her, why had he expected anything more?

CHAPTER 13

Quution twitched in his sleep. A tickling sensation ran down his neck. He brushed at his ear and winced when his claw shredded the sensitive skin of his lobe.

He blinked his eyes open. What had woken him?

An inhale sent alarms through him. He sat up and twisted around. Why wasn't Xan's scent stronger?

He searched for her prone form. Her corner was empty.

Jumping up, he ran around the library as if he couldn't see it in its entirety by standing in one spot.

Xan was nowhere to be found.

How had she snuck out? His energy and Stryke's together should've trapped any being.

He lurched out of the room. Where could she have gone? He charged down the corridor before coming to a halt.

What was he doing? He could follow her anywhere.

He dragged in a slow breath to force his heart rate to calm. Vibrations trailed over his skin. Her energy pattern was fading.

Spinning on his heel, he stormed in the other direction.

She couldn't have gotten that far ahead of him. Her passing through his wards had to be what had woken him.

A familiar presence appeared behind him. He didn't bother turning around. "I have her trail."

"How'd she get out?" Stryke growled, pulling even with him in the passageway.

Quution glanced over and did a double take. Stryke's tight shirt had a cartoon cat with hearts for eyes. The blue plaid flannel pajama pants were more his style, at least.

Stryke shot him a glare. "It's Zoey's shirt. It was dark."

"Why wear clothing at all?"

"It's become a habit. Besides, the shirt is already on. I'm not tossing it and risking her wrath."

Xan's scent called to him, her energy a fine, glittery filigree in the air. Quution powered around corner after corner. She'd made good use of her short time of freedom.

Stryke stopped. "We've circled around this spot three times. I can't smell her."

Quution didn't stop. "She's close." Two more turns. Three, tops.

Stryke's footsteps raced closer. He yanked on Quution's elbow.

Quution wrenched his arm out of Stryke's grasp. "What are you doing, Brother? She's close."

Stryke grabbed him again. "Is she? Or is she messing with you again?"

She wouldn't do that... But the words died on his lips. He studied his surroundings. Stryke was right. He had taken lefts over and over again and circled back. The library was around the corner.

He fisted his hands and hissed at the sharp points of his claws. He kept his voice low. "She can't be far away. Her powers must require proximity." They had to, because then it'd mean he could still find her.

"Let me try." Stryke slid him a sidelong glance. "She doesn't hold quite the influence over me."

Stryke scanned the corridor as he turned right and left, swiveling backward and forward. He stared back where they'd come from, where Quution had originally run.

The crafty vixen.

He picked up speed until they were jogging. His uneven platforms sent shocks through his spine. He brushed away the discomfort and ignored the strong urge to trot in the opposite direction.

She wasn't fooling him again.

As they pursued Xan, he couldn't help but wonder why, during all her time tricking him, she hadn't tried to assassinate him. Surely her master would consider a dead Quution a good Quution.

Was it the risk of failure?

No, she had to know he couldn't hurt her. She'd duped him into revealing his real self, cooking for her, and then making love to her in his bed, where he would've given everything to her. And after that deception was revealed, he'd still offered her his sandwich and given her one of his favorite books.

She'd first bargained with him to read in exchange for not spilling the secret of how he'd been raised and his relationship to Stryke. Could she be spying on him because her master had a hold on her?

The sister. And the niece.

Xan wasn't one of the typical evil demons roaming the underworld. She'd killed her mama for her sister's safety. What was a little seduction and espionage compared to that if she needed to save her family again?

Her scent curled around him like a finger crooking him in her direction.

"Xan!" he roared and picked up his speed. Stryke called

his name, but Quution spotted a slinky, purple-tinted shadow skirting the wall of the passage.

He flailed for all the energy he could gather and tossed it out in the form of a net. Xan stopped, her body rigid, a strangled noise escaping her.

He'd unintentionally given her an electrical shock. Backing off on the energy, he rushed the rest of the way to her.

"I'm sorry" were the first words out of his mouth.

A pinch of anger drained from her gaze. "That hurt."

"I didn't mean—you were getting away."

Stryke huffed up next to him. "Sweet brimstone, she's the escapee. Don't fucking apologize."

Instead of snarling at Stryke, Xan lifted her chin, her face haughty. "That's why Quution's the sexy brother."

"Your game's off," Stryke replied. "Who's sexier isn't one of my concerns."

She slid her gaze away. "I wasn't appealing to *your* fear."

"It isn't mine," Quution sputtered.

Xan lifted a dark brow.

He shook his head. She had them twisted around less than thirty seconds after they'd captured her. "You really are good."

"Apparently not," she muttered. "Or you wouldn't keep trapping me."

"We muck up a bit when our loved ones are in trouble. Don't we?" He hoped she'd talk to him this time. Between him and Stryke, even Melody, they could help her. They could help her family.

"What are you talking about?" Xan couldn't meet his gaze.

"Xera. Xoda. Who's using them to get you to work for them?"

❧

XAN WAS AT A CROSSROADS, but it wasn't which corridor to sprint down to lose the demon brothers. She wanted to trust Quution so badly. He knew she had a sister and a niece and she should've kept that info to herself. Quution was nothing like Spaeth, but in reality, how well did she know him?

When his back was to the wall, how did she know he wouldn't use her?

He'd pointed out how astonishing her ability was, and she'd learned the hard way what demons would do to secure her cooperation. Her dilemma wasn't only about Quution. Stryke's perplexed gaze darted between her and Quution.

"Let me rephrase. Who has your sister and niece?"

"There's more of her?" Stryke asked.

Yes, there were, though her kind didn't hang out and have family reunions, and births were few and far between. Their coloring was part of their camouflage, and they stayed hidden. A low-key lifestyle was necessary to prevent abduction, forced breeding, or—she repressed a shudder—their addition to the pile of bones in the sacrificial cave.

She'd done a good job for herself, until Spaeth had found her somehow. Now, she was on the freaking Circle. It was the complete opposite of lying low. And that was despite missing every gathering possible and not mingling with the others.

"We can help them," Quution said.

She still hadn't spoken. Understanding was dawning on Stryke. He didn't look happy his brother was caving, but it'd lead to the answer they were seeking.

But Quution didn't follow up his offer with an ultimatum. He wasn't coercing her, bargaining with her, or blackmailing her. Yes, they would lock her back into the empty half of the library, probably in chains this time, but she couldn't fault them. Their lives were in danger too. Spaeth would whip the entire underworld into a frenzy until each and every demon down here was hunting the brothers.

And their troubles weren't isolated to this realm. Stryke's mate and everyone she cared about would be threatened as well.

Yet, Quution genuinely wanted to help her. He gave no indication otherwise.

She glanced around the dim caves. No one was close, but one could never be sure. "Let's go back to the library."

Quution nodded and stepped to the side to allow her to pass first.

Xan kept her shoulders back as she walked, but she really wanted to hunch over and drag her feet. Spaeth was harmless in that he was predictably evil. If Quution got her to trust him, then let her down? That seemed so much worse.

But her mission wasn't as cut and dried as she'd thought. Bug Quution, collect information, tattle on him, and then find Xera and get her to safety. Now she'd have to bank on Spaeth not finding any of them, or she'd have to test her skills to the maximum and fight him. Things just got more complicated.

Back in the library, she deliberately traipsed over to Quution's side and sat in his chair. She crossed her legs. Stryke leaned against the entrance and crossed his arms. It was her first good look at him today.

"Nice shirt," she said.

His stolid expression didn't flicker. "Thanks."

It was becoming clearer why she liked him despite his attitude toward her. He wasn't unnecessarily cruel, a rare trait in this realm. His care for Quution was obvious too. How did they hide that they were related? Most minions were openly hostile and full of resentment over their circumstances, but Stryke had never acted like that. And he didn't ogle or leer at her, even behind her back. She could be wandering around in snow pants and a parka and he wouldn't look at her any differently.

Quution shuffled to the desk. The more she thought about what he was planning, the more she wondered why the getup. Sure, full-bloods would scorn him, but they'd be even less concerned that he posed a serious threat if they thought he was half as strong. His reasoning didn't make any sense.

They waited for her to start talking. Mellow, unhurried, no sense of belligerence. Perhaps that was the reason she finally told them what they wanted to hear.

"Spaeth."

No rage roiled out of them. Quution exchanged a charged lilac glance with Stryke's violet one. The name came as no surprise to them, but would any full-breed have really been a shocker?

"I don't know where he's keeping them. The deal was that I find out what you're up to and he'd release my family. I have three days left."

Quution's brow dropped as he thought through her predicament. Stryke gave her a *do you really think Spaeth will keep his word?* look.

"I'm not a rookie," she said defensively. "I know Spaeth will either refuse to release them and keep me under his power or find some other way to control me. Prolonging the situation was my first goal, but recently, he's been putting a lot of pressure on me and I haven't gotten a vibe of where they are."

"We can work together," Quution offered. "We'll help you find them."

"And then what? It's not as if I back your stupid idea to trap us all down here."

Stryke pushed off the doorframe. "You two argue that out. I'm going to search the underworld and see if I can pinpoint where Spaeth's chamber is and where he's keeping your family prisoner."

"Finding them isn't going to make me so grateful I'll keep quiet about your wards."

Quution's expression remained placid. "Maybe finding them will convince you why we need to take extreme measures to keep a demon like Spaeth in this realm."

"Or," Stryke cut in, "maybe I'm a decent guy and won't let a female and her child suffer."

Quution's steady gaze didn't leave hers. "That too."

"Meanwhile, *I'm* still a prisoner." They were helping free her family while she was their captive.

Quution's mouth tightened. "No, but I ask that we join teams, at least temporarily."

It was her only out—for now. "Temporarily." When Xera and Xoda were free, she'd take off with them, head deep into unexplored caverns.

Xoda would love…

What would she love?

Stryke interrupted her thoughts. "I'll stop in tomorrow. Buzz me if you need anything, Q."

In other words, call him if she caused trouble. She almost rolled her eyes, but she was alone in a room with Quution, a room she supposedly could leave at any time.

CHAPTER 14

Quution regarded the female sitting mutinously in his chair. She had to see the logic in warding the underworld. He shuddered to think what Spaeth had done to Xera, or worse, the little girl. Using her family's situation to support his argument wasn't appropriate, and it wasn't relevant anyway. All his work would do was limit Spaeth's reach to the underworld.

Which would be a major improvement for many demons. He had to get Xan to see that. "If the full-bloods didn't need half-breeds to do their bidding in the human realm, there would be no need to enslave them."

While half-breeds could possess a human without their muted powers blowing the host's circuit, it was notoriously difficult for a pure-blooded demon to possess a being in the other realm. They needed a powerful host like an elite vampire, and if Demetrius and his team were successful at their jobs, that'd become next to impossible.

But Xan didn't appear to be swayed. The fingers of one arm tapped the surface of the desk. One long leg was crossed over the other, her foot bobbing until he felt like he was under interrogation.

"Do you know what it's like to work for a powerful demon?"

He'd never had the misfortune. "Pain and torture."

She lifted a shoulder. "For some. For others, it's a haven. A powerful being watching out for you." She uncrossed her legs and sat forward. "But you know what else they provide?"

His mind was still turning over her claim that being controlled was a haven. How could it be?

But then he thought of the lesser half-breeds, the ones with wimpy powers and mediocre fighting skills. It'd be like the mafia. A mob-boss demon protecting them. A name to throw around to fend off the baddies.

She didn't wait for him to answer. "They're our access to the human realm. To television. To good food that doesn't try to eat us first. To massages and moonlit strolls and a fine merlot."

He processed her words but couldn't reconcile them with the demons he knew. "They find a host and destroy the host's life with less concern than they would have for a bug. The only goal of having a host, for most demons, is to find a route for easier possession, to find a strong vampire for their full-blooded master."

"Is that what you do?" she challenged.

"You know I don't." He'd always prided himself in how he treated his hosts, but he couldn't deny the times he'd gotten them into grave danger—or shot.

"Oh." She nodded, but it was an overexaggerated motion. "You're like the unicorn of demons. Only *you* would treat a host right, as if possessing them wasn't an ultimate violation in the first place. But they should be thankful when you possess them. The rest of us? Evil monsters."

"How did you find Marcus?"

"His cult-loving ex-girlfriend summoned the full-breed I was working with. I'm sorry, the full-breed Malachi was repeatedly mauling when he was alive and who wanted a way out. I was tasked with finding a host strong enough for her." She reclined in the chair and draped one leg over the other. "But it proved difficult with the Circle cronies recruiting their own vampires to possess and take over the realm. She was killed before I could finish. My deal with her was over, but I kept Marcus."

He would've, too. A self-sufficient human with few ties to other humans outside of work left Xan days where she could gallivant around in him without raising suspicion from those who cared about him.

He conceded the point she'd made, but only slightly. "You and I are different. I've seen the swath of destruction other demons have left. People suffer. Families are destroyed. The violations are both personal and physical. It's sickening. If we keep on this path, both full-bloods and half-breeds alike will find a way to bring hell on Earth."

"You don't think highly of our kind."

He threw his hands in the air, his long claws glinting in the torchlight. "How could I think any other way? I was born into captivity. My mother was neglectful on a good day, which was rare. I did not want her attention. You killed your mother to protect your sister, and you're spying on me to protect your living relatives. Sounds like a fine species to let gallivant wherever they want."

Xan ran her tongue across her teeth, managing not to nick a fang. He wanted to lick along that fang, watch her shiver from his touch.

He steeled himself. The heavy discussion should be muting his libido, but alas, around Xan, that was never the case.

"Being in a host like Marcus is the only joy I've ever

known. There is no joy down here."

Her words sent him reeling. No, there wasn't any joy to be had in the underworld. But his memories kept trying to yank him back to the time with her in his chamber, when she'd...

That had been fake.

"And the real question," she continued, "is how stuck down here with us would you be? Hypocritical, don't you think? Confine the rest of us, but only after you figure out how to move freely."

Dare he tell her? "Two demons I care very much about have mates in the human realm. I will not separate them."

"And you?"

He couldn't answer. His motivations aligned with hers. There was no joy in the underworld, but in humans, their energy—their love, their passion, their *fun*... He wasn't leaving it behind.

He'd thought he felt it all on a different level because of his energy. Yet Xan spoke like she'd plucked the words of his favorite host experiences from his head.

"So taking it away from everyone else is fine. Got it." Xan rose, her lithe body graceful. "I have my sister to find."

"If you or I go looking, Spaeth will know something's up. He gave you a deadline and he'll wonder why you aren't pushing for answers."

"Oh, I've gotten answers. I could go to him now."

"You said you'd work with me." Temporarily.

"You haven't made a good case for why I should."

At least she wasn't leaving. The way she strolled through his wards, he didn't know if he could contain her, or if he wanted to damage her trust more. Her acceptance didn't matter; it was what he had to do.

"I'm not just being selfish. Someone needs to oversee the wards, make sure that they're holding and perform regular maintenance." He went for full disclosure. "The vampires, they're the first, dare I say, friends I've ever had. Stryke is my only family. You have your sister and your niece. Would they tolerate me?"

His real talk was enough to capture her attention. "You trust vampires over me?"

"Does it matter who I trust? But, yes, they have earned my trust."

Had she gotten closer? "And naturally, you've taken it upon yourself to be the hall monitor."

"A realm monitor, yes."

"Quution the All-Powerful."

He frowned. "No."

"Quution the Magnanimous."

He shook his head. "It's not like tha—"

"Quution the—"

"What else am I going to do?" he snapped. He tried to shove his hand through his hair, but two of his claws caught his forehead. He growled and a ripped both offending claws off, then picked away at the other three, tossing them on the floor.

"And me? What about me?"

She had slinked closer. All his claws were off. If he touched her, he wouldn't mar her soft skin. "I'm just your job."

Regret crossed her face. "You're not *just* a job."

But he was her target. "I'm a means to an end. The…what we did…all that was an illusion. You didn't mean any of it." He tried to say that neither had he, but he couldn't tell such a bold lie.

"Do you recall the part of the fantasy where you thought I was sick?"

He forced himself to go back to that day. Avoidance had been key to keep from distracting himself. He could surrender himself to the delusion and not reemerge for anyone. It'd been that good. But, yes, he did remember concern over her well-being.

"I made myself look like that host you use."

"Why?" He hadn't chosen the host because she was attractive. Brooklyn's stress over college graduation made her a beacon to a demon like him.

"Because I thought that was what you liked. Call me surprised when I dropped my personal mirage and you were fine." She stepped into his personal space. "So, what about me, Quution?"

"I still don't understand your question. I'm just a job for you."

Anger sparked in her purple gaze. "Do you think I fuck my targets?" Her fury swelled and she was turning away.

He panicked and grabbed her arm. "Don't go." She stopped, but the tremor running through her said he was still on shaky ground. "What am I to think? I'm not your type. My *power* is coveted, not me. Are you…" Was he a fool for asking? "Do you like me?"

Had he possessed so many humans that he was tying himself in knots trying to figure out his feelings?

"I wanted to fuck you so bad I still ache."

The sonic boom of her claim disappeared under a swell of desire. His hands were on her waist before his conscious mind could come back online.

"You…did?" Because he did, too. "Then why didn't you?" He would've been more than a willing participant, and if Stryke had visited and interrupted him while he was inside of Xan, Stryke's life would've been in grave danger.

"Like you said, it was all fake. Your reasons for wanting me were under false pretenses."

"But this is real."

"I guess it is. So, what do we do about it?"

He was swamped in her scent. Lavender with the smell of home he'd thought he hated so much. His hands were on her warm body. A little tug and she'd be curved into him.

A pink tongue darted out to lick her lips and her gaze was on his mouth.

Today seemed the day for honesty. He went with it. "I know what I want to do."

"Me too."

Okay. This was going to happen. She had a few days left before she was to report to Spaeth. Stryke wasn't coming back until tomorrow, and to keep up the ruse, she was supposed to be seducing him.

But he'd never done this before. Her previous partners had probably been experienced, even a little brutish—or a lot brutish. Quution didn't know what she liked, but—

She wrapped one hand around each fang and yanked. A flash of pain burst through his mouth, but his prosthetics released without bloodshed. His real, smaller fangs held strong.

She dumped the fakes on the floor next to his "claws." "Those are ridiculous." Her gaze rose to his. "But they grew on me. I just want them out of my way."

Her gaze heated and she kissed the spots on his lips that were still indented from his falsies.

His pulse hammered through his ears. "You were my biggest annoyance. But I looked for you around every corner."

He tightened his grip and bent his head. As soon as his lips touched hers and she returned the pressure, he was lost.

He swung her around until her ass hit the desktop. Lifting her on top, he stepped between her legs. Leaning over her more than if she were standing, he briefly wondered if she would mind.

But she wrapped her legs around his waist and hugged his

shoulders so tightly he couldn't have backed away even if he'd wanted to.

He plundered her hot, wet mouth. The only things between them were his ratty clothes, but he refused to pull back enough to get them off.

He'd rather have her tear them off.

She must've had the same idea. The next moment, his jacket was yanked down his arms, pinning them to his sides, his hands on her legs.

Pulling away, she purred, "Ooh, I think I like this."

He did too. But no way was he going to miss using his hands during his first time with a female. Not with *this* female.

Shrugging the coat off the rest of the way, it hit the floor at his boots.

The shoes would have to go. He snaked an arm around her and captured her mouth again as he toed out of his bulky footwear. Kicking them off, he dropped a couple of inches in height, bringing her center even with his.

His loose pants didn't inhibit his erection. It prodded her core and she rubbed against him.

A low groan resonated through his chest and into hers.

Seams tore as she ripped his shirt off, but it didn't slow them down. Their mouths clashed. She stroked her tongue against his. He sucked on it, on her lips, until she nicked his tender flesh with a fang.

He planted his hands on the desktop, sagging from the pleasure, his moan echoing through the chamber. She broke away from him with a sultry, wicked smile.

"Do it again," he said, his voice ragged.

"Where?" she whispered and yanked at his pants. The cloth tie snapped. His pants floated down his legs. He shoved them away with a foot.

He was naked with Xan and this time it wasn't a fantasy.

This was real.

He looked down between them. His thick erection prodded her belly.

She caught his lower lip with her fang, sending another shot of electricity to his groin and making his erection jump. He held his breath as she ran a finger along his length, the intimate, light stroke enough to send tremors down his spine.

He wasn't going to ravage her like a…well, like a demon. She could set the pace and he'd do his best to keep up.

She swirled her finger around the tip of his cock. He wasn't prepared for her fist to close around him.

"Xan." His eyelids drifted shut as he rocked into her grip.

But she didn't pump him, she guided him to her hot entrance.

His eyelids flew up. "Don't you need to… Shouldn't we…" Why did he get tongue-tied talking about sex? But he'd learned enough to know that foreplay was critical.

"Shouldn't we what, Quution?" she asked innocently. But she was naughty with his shaft, rubbing it up and down her seam. "Don't I feel ready?"

She did. Her wetness coated his tip, and searing heat branded her scent into him. "Yes," he said through clenched teeth.

She spread her legs farther, her heels digging into his hips. His gaze was riveted to her core, open for him.

She placed him at her center and caught his gaze. Molten passion flowed through her eyes and her lips were parted. "Do it."

He grabbed her hips and thrust forward. His head fell back and a jagged groan left him as he slid into her inch by inch.

Her panted breaths reached him as he gazed at where her swollen flesh encased his cock. So damn erotic.

He wasn't fully seated inside, but he didn't keep pushing forward. Rocking out, he took his time penetrating her again.

Her low moan stroked his male ego. Already his balls were tightening, energy coiling at the base of his spine like it was demanding he thrust, thrust, thrust. It was what they both wanted.

She rocked her hips until he was buried within her. He held her still. Her walls rippled around him, gripping up and down his length.

Amazing. There was no pleasure in the human realm that could match this.

She caressed the side of his face and breathed his name. If he'd thought he was lost before, he was done for now. Swinging his hips, he drove into her over and over again. He grunted from the waves of ecstasy crashing into him. She hung on to him, matching his rhythm.

The instinct to please his female kicked in. He licked his thumb and circled her clit. She cried out and fell back, slamming her hands into the desktop to catch herself.

He stroked the outside of her nub and angled his hips up to hit her zone from the inside. A flood of heat covered his hand as her walls clamped down on his shaft. She arched her back, his name rolling off her lips.

His own orgasm hit and it was nothing like their fantasy date. Coming inside of her was a state of bliss he'd never thought possible. Nothing like this had been in his research. The closeness, the rapture, the connection. Wet, hot satin wrapped around his cock, milking him until he hung over her, their foreheads touching.

He couldn't talk, he could barely catch his breath.

Xan laid a soft kiss on the corner of his mouth. "Did any of your research tell you that demons have amazing stamina and can fuck for days?"

CHAPTER 15

*S*he'd created a monster. A delicious-looking monster with a chiseled ass and abs she could sharpen daggers on.

Two days later, she was pinned over the desk, much like they'd started, only this time her feet were firmly braced on the floor, spread enough to open her to Quution's exquisitely punishing thrusts. The cool desktop was the only thing keeping her from combusting.

Each time he drove inside, a gasp, moan, groan, or grunt escaped her. And the shameless demon had learned to use his energy ability while fucking.

There was nothing like a gentle shock to the clit while a cock was buried inside to get a girl off.

He was doing it now. A constant buzz at her core, until her muscles constricted and her orgasm slammed into her.

"Quution!" she hollered, used to her voice echoing off the walls. She'd lost count of the number of times she'd come. Her voice ought to be hoarse, but she always managed to heal just in time for the next screaming climax.

Somehow, she registered his rigid body behind her and

his release spilling hot, sparking inside of her. He was a live wire and it strung out her own orgasm until she worried her heart would stop.

Finishing, he slumped over her, peppering her shoulders with kisses. She pried her hands off the far edge of the desk and twisted enough to meet his lips.

They tasted of her and the candy bugs they feasted on between rounds of sex, when he snuggled her into his jacket and curled around her.

And like each time before, no matter where they'd copulated, he lifted her into his arms and crossed to the corner that she now considered theirs.

She was swaddled in his clothing, his strong arms around her, her eyelids drooping, when he said, "Stryke should be here soon."

"Mm." She could nap until then. She doubted he'd found anything.

The energy demon hadn't had any more luck than Xan had in locating Xera. Spaeth had been lying unusually low, but the Circle wasn't very active at the moment. All seats were filled and no one wanted to incite an event that could get them killed. Or they were like Quution, off planning an event that could get them killed.

"How old is Xoda again?"

She squirmed to get more comfortable. He'd asked every day they'd been in here. Had she always fallen asleep before she answered? "Seven or so. I wasn't there when she was born."

The day Xera had surprised her with a wiggly purple baby had been one of Xan's best. A member of the family, free from corruption. A girl they could raise to be the best of them. It was like her dream had come true.

"Yesterday, you said she was ten or so."

"Yep. Around there." Did it matter? They lived so long the years blended into each other.

"But Xera is seventy-eight."

"Yep. Two-hundred and twenty years younger than me."

"Mm."

Her lips twitched. He'd picked up her habit. Sleep claimed her until she awoke to male voices.

"I can't find a thing," Stryke said, his tone low. He'd used her own energy pattern like a signal and he was the receiver, and he'd gone hunting for an energy signature with similar patterns to hers. "I get on a trail and then I get this constant, gnawing anxiety until I have to leave to go find Zoey. She's irritated because I keep tracking her down in the middle of a mission, or waking her up, but I have to put my hands on her before the feeling dulls even a little."

"And that's Xera's trail?" Quution asked.

"No. Spaeth's. I can't even get a bead on Xera without ending up in a corner, shaking. I've imagined Zoey killed a hundred different ways," Stryke hissed. "I can't search for Xera anymore."

"And the niece?"

Xan opened her eyes in time for Stryke to answer. "No trail. They're exceptional at covering their tracks."

"Maybe he doesn't have her," Quution replied from behind the desk they'd had sex on too many times to count.

She lied, it was six times.

Stryke paced across from his brother. His normally handsome face was haggard. Dark circles hung under his eyes and his gaze was tired.

"Spaeth's making Xera protect him." She should've come to the conclusion earlier. "I'm sure he's coercing her with my safety like he's doing to me with her."

"And Xoda," Quution added, but he watched her closely, his gaze oddly intent.

"Where Xera is, she'll have Xoda." Her singular pride was raising her sister to care for a young. Xan rose fluidly to her feet. "I need to be the one looking for her."

Stryke pinched the bridge of his nose. "Normally, I'd argue, but I'm not getting anywhere."

Quution ducked his head. "We'll search. You go, get some rest. Xan's deadline is up in a day and we'll need to be fully rested to face Spaeth."

The brothers were on her side. She'd made the right decision in telling them. If Spaeth was using her sister's powers, then it was no wonder Xan hadn't found her.

Stryke shuffled out, muttering that he'd be there when they needed him.

Quution slid his gaze away from the empty doorway to her. Their time in the library turned sex den was over.

"I need to stop at my chamber." He gestured to the pile of claws and fangs. "I need my glue."

He still insisted on his deception, thinking it helped. She wouldn't argue. If he was helping her, they didn't need the extra attention anyway.

Quution pressed the final claw on and held it until the glue set. "Where will you meet Spaeth?"

"He'll summon me." Xan reclined on his stone slab bed, and it was hard not to ditch his task and take her on every surface of his place. But they needed to pick up where Stryke had left off. "I'm a little surprised he waited the whole week. He was getting antsy."

And Quution had been getting close to cementing the final ward he'd need to allow him to pass through. Ironically, Xan had completely derailed him, which would delight Spaeth before her deception enraged him.

Quution wouldn't let that happen. Spaeth wasn't going to damage one patch of purple skin on Xan's body.

The glue dry, he palpated his fangs. The sweet relief of having had them off for days was gone. His platform shoes were back on, his trench coat in place. At least this time it smelled of Xan's fresh fragrance.

Could he find a way to bring her scent with him when it was time to go? He couldn't ask her to abandon her family, and he couldn't bring them with. He had a responsibility that transcended his lust.

"I am ready." He rolled his neck to work the kinks out before he lurched around the underworld in his uneven boots.

Her gaze swept over him. A moment of insecurity flitted through him. Usually, it was the other way around. His real form was the vulnerable one down here. Dressed like this, with the rumors of his power to back him up, he was feared. Without it, he'd walk around like Stryke, getting eyed for future enslavement.

Stryke had his protection, not that he needed it. But if his brother had to spend his days in the underworld, enslavement would be a constant danger. With his powers and his half-breed status, Stryke would always be a target.

Xan's bland expression was the equivalent of "Mm." She strode out the door. He followed her, securing the wood plank behind him.

"Stryke couldn't sense her energy," he said. "How have you looked for Xera?"

And Xoda, but there was something odd about the niece that he couldn't place. Xan was different when she gushed about the girl, but not in the way he'd expect. She was so specific when she talked about Xera, but with Xoda, there was a vagueness that didn't sit well with him. Yet, what would he know? It wasn't like there were happy families roaming all over the realm.

Xan turned into a whole different demon when speaking about Xoda. Shouldn't she know her niece's exact age?

Xan was getting ahead of him, discussing her method of searching the underworld. He shuffled to keep up, keeping his gaze north of her swaying ass.

"Spaeth keeps his lair hidden better than most," she said. "But I suspect he always meets me close to where he hides. He's not a popular guy, and it isn't just his radioactive personality."

"I've long suspected him of burning demons who go up against him." They turned a few corners, and Quution waited to continue until he sensed the passageways before them were empty. "But all I have are random piles of ashes and his lingering energy. No proof." And as long as he hadn't crossed paths with the demon, Quution hadn't cared.

But Spaeth had put Xan in his way. How many others like Xan had Spaeth destroyed? The full-blooded demon was a good example of why the wards were necessary.

"I'm sure it was him. He's probably eating babies with the rest of them."

Quution stopped like he'd hit a wall. "How do you know about that?"

Xan glanced over her shoulder and did a double take when she noticed he was several feet behind. "Is it, like, a big secret?" She snapped her fingers. "Right. You still have it all sealed."

"How'd you get in?" She knew about the sacrifices of the young to harvest power. She knew how to get into the chamber. Those weren't his wards. The high he'd been on since being in Xan's arms plummeted.

"I can always get through. And I didn't bring it up because

I found your childhood cell and sensed it was better to use that against you."

"What would you have done with the info?"

She gave him a *hello?* look. "Used it to get my way." She narrowed her eyes. "I still don't sense that it's a huge fear to you that the existence of a baby sacrificing room gets out." She peered harder. "Only that I kept my knowledge of it from you. What the hell do you think I would do with a pile of bones?"

Her defensive tone was enough to get him to back off. "Not you. They don't know that I know and I'd planned to use it against them."

"Understandable. But in the meantime, do you let them sacrifice away?"

He liked the disapproving note in her voice. She would've done as she said and used the info to her advantage. But she wasn't involved.

"I've set my energy lines around the wards. I'll know if someone enters." Except for her. His energy happily let her through anywhere. "After the loss of Hypna and the upheaval of the Circle, I think those involved backed off."

"And do you know those involved?"

He shook his head. "I assume all full-bloods are guilty." Power-hungry bastards. Breeding and killing to harvest powers. "And those halflings associated with them, whether voluntarily or not. They need to be stopped."

"When the guilty parties learn what you plan, they'll double down."

"Ah." Quution couldn't believe he was revealing his plan, but he didn't want her to think he'd intentionally make life worse down here—beyond what was needed for the realm wards. "But once I carry out my plan, the wards around the altar room will drop, and I have it arranged for the Circle to learn about the sacrifices."

"And the half-breeds will wreak havoc and go on a rampage, thereby taking the focus off you and your wards while you escape." She shook her head. "You're a devious bastard and it's turning me on."

He'd do something about that against the wall, but they were on a mission, one that didn't promise to be easy if Stryke had failed.

"What are my weaknesses?" he asked.

"Excuse me?"

Had no one ever asked her that? "Stryke couldn't find Xera because she got to him through his mate. He knew it was happening and still couldn't fight it. But if I can alert you to sudden fears or overwhelming anxiety, maybe we can team up against her powers." He had no doubt he could find Xera from her energy, but getting close to her was proving to be the issue.

Xan nodded but stayed silent. Instead, as she looked at him, he had the sense of being flayed open, dissected, and it had nothing to do with her power. Her perusal was open and blatant. Her targets probably felt antsy when she eyed them, like he did now, but otherwise had no clue that their personalities and past experiences were being studied and inspected in a unique way that would be their undoing.

"You fear discovery," she finally said.

The word "stop" was on the tip of his tongue. Were these details he really wanted to know? When he'd first asked, he'd wondered who *wouldn't* want to know. Knowledge was power and learning one's own weak points was the ultimate advantage in building one's defenses. But the dread running through him was akin to being told when and how he would die.

She continued. "You hide your origins, you hide your true nature, and you hide your studies. The reasons are plentiful, which only gives them more power."

"And they are?" he croaked. She hadn't gotten to his true weakness. Was that because she was trying to hide the extent of how well she could peer into him? Or because she could sense his escalating discomfort?

She drew in a breath before she spoke. "Insecurity. Your greatest fear is that you're not good enough." Her pause sent his heart thumping. "It's why you like the human realm. You're *more than* up there, all while having a valid excuse to hide who you are."

Her gaze slid away. Faint disappointment resonated from her. "No happiness. Overwhelming love for your brother and concern for your friends. So Xera will likely inspire panic that a horde is after you, or that you're being laughed at. Maybe something like the story about humans with Frankenstein. Or she'll target those you care about."

Oh. Well, that didn't seem so bad. "And you turned all that into a placid cabin by the lake?" She amazed him more every day. "I'm prepared, and I'll find her."

He'd meant to be reassuring, but she watched him with near indifference. Had he let her down by allowing her to view the real him?

CHAPTER 16

Xan couldn't hide her disappointment. Quution was surprisingly well adjusted. Everyone's past shaped them, and his mother had hidden him, abused him, and neglected him, but she'd also molded a strong demon with a solid sense of self, and Xan didn't need to be a full-range empath to know that.

His personal horror was not being good enough. And that bothered her. What had she expected? That her well-being would be his top fear? That the two days they'd spent together would endear her so much to him that she displaced fears that had been formed when he was a kid?

Still, a girl could hope. She liked him, liked being with him, but she didn't mean enough to him to register as more than a mild concern. She couldn't view herself as a worry to him at all.

And when had she thought he'd be anything more than a demon in matters of the heart? He was leaving the realm, abandoning everyone in here. Which to be honest, she'd do in a blink. But she had Xera and…and Xoda. As long as her family was stuck here, there was no use trying to figure out how she could ride Quution's coattails on out.

He swept through the corridors ahead of her. The buzz of his energy rippled over her skin and it wasn't even aimed at her. She was that attuned to him.

And she meant nothing to him. A means to an end? A way to get to Spaeth? Quution was goal oriented, after all.

She shook off her thoughts. They weren't helping and the focus now was on her sister. And Xoda.

Xan's heart clenched. She tried to summon her niece's image, but it was hazy. Xera's was clear as a bell. Same dark eyes, same smooth scalp. Xera was a little taller, her overall appeal a little more...vicious. Perhaps it was her longer fangs, or the resting bitch face. Xera was stone-cold. For several years, Xan had worried she hadn't gotten to her in time.

But Xoda. She was everything sweet about their kind. Her laugh was…

Xan frowned. Still, she couldn't summon the memory. Usually it came to her at random times. Xoda's giggle, her attempts at summoning candy beetles. But Xan couldn't clearly recall any of those instances.

It had to be the stress.

She stalled in her tracks. What if something terrible had befallen Xoda? Could her memories of Xoda be foggy because her niece was gone?

A strangled sound escaped her throat.

Quution spun around immediately. "What is it?"

Xan's mouth worked before she spoke. "Xoda."

His brows lowered as he figured out what she meant. "You're upset about her?"

Xan nodded, tears burning the backs of her eyes. She never cried. Never. "You're following Xera's energy signature. Do you sense two of them, one for Xoda?"

Quution's face was grim. "I do not. But that doesn't mean

what you think." He lurched toward her, his eyes wary, like he was afraid to say what was on his mind. "Do you think, perhaps, Xera is using your love for Xoda to keep you from finding her?"

"What? *No.*" Xera wouldn't. That would be deplorable.

"Not even to save their lives? We don't know how Spaeth's using them."

Talking it out with Quution was helping. Her heart rate slowed. Her eyes dried. Xera was crafty. Ruthless, needlessly so at times. "It's possible."

Xera could be throwing off Xan's power to keep her away. Xoda was an obvious and effective target. Yes, that made sense. The lack of memories would fuel her intense fear for her family.

"Are you feeling any effects?" she asked.

He shook his head. "Can she only target one at a time?"

"To be that defined, yes." Unless, like the demons she'd sent chasing an imaginary food source to keep from eating her, a group shared the same ultimate goal. She and Quution had the same goal, but he hadn't met Xera, or Xoda either. No one had. They'd kept her a secret.

Quution ducked his head to peer at her, grasping her shoulders. His warm touch was grounding. "Are you ready to continue?"

"Yes." A glow burned in her belly from his concern. But she had to remind herself that Xera was a way to keep Spaeth from interfering with his wards.

Quution took twists and turns deep into the underworld, far away from where she'd ever searched.

An impending sense of doom dogged her, and Xoda was central in her thoughts. Each time Xan tried to imagine Xoda's dark eyes, she saw her sister's. Each time she tried to recall Xoda's laugh, it was Xera's husky voice that floated through her mind.

But she pushed through. Quution's words had made sense.

As soon as the heavy weight of dread lifted from her shoulders, Quution stumbled. He looked around.

Xera was targeting him now.

Dismay snaked through her. Her sister had used her own kid against Xan. That seemed so…low.

But it was to keep them safe. *We don't know how Spaeth is using them.* Again, Quution was right.

Xera had gained power. She'd always been exceptional, and thanks to Xan's redirection, she wasn't another mindless demon stricken with a cruel streak.

Quution's steps stuttered again. He snapped his head one way, then another.

"What do you think you hear?" There was no noise in this area. The bugs in the walls were quiet and this area of the underworld had probably been abandoned before Xera was imprisoned here.

"My mother."

"She's dead, Quution." Xan had to be blunt. Truth was key to thwarting these thoughts and feelings. Manipulation made the fears bloom.

"I know. The only thing I can thank my sire for."

"How did she die?" If she could get him talking, the emotions inside of him would be forced aside by the truth of his words.

"Slowly and painfully. She survived my sire's attack enough to birth me. There was little energy around to help her heal. She was weak for years. Feeble, but mean. Eventually, she expired, and…"

His throat worked like he was trying not to throw up.

"And?" she pressed.

He swallowed and shook himself. "I, um, had to live off

the bugs that cleaned her bones." A cough escaped, but he'd masked the sound of a gag.

She sucked in a breath. Her first thought was that Quution had been fortunate the bugs had waited until his mother had passed. The creatures in this realm were cannibals, opportunists, scavengers, whatever worked for survival. To eat the same critters that had… Ick.

"That explains the human food."

He bobbed his head as if he was afraid to open his mouth or he'd upchuck the sandwiches Stryke had been bringing them.

"Do you hear her anymore?"

He let out a gusty breath. "No."

She wound her arm through his. His muscles were strung tight, but he shuffled along. Occasionally, his gaze would dart around, but he didn't stop again.

"We're getting close," he said gruffly.

She'd been misled. He was struggling more than she'd thought, but he hid it well.

He was growing tenser by the second until she didn't know how he was able to move his legs. Veins standing out in his neck, his jaw set, he plowed forward.

"Talk to me—" She snapped her head around.

Xera was nearby. Her sister's scent was all over this corridor, unusually strong. It was as thick as Xan's was in the library, but only because she'd been sexing Quution for days.

Her heart climbed into her throat. Had Spaeth—

No. Xan didn't sense fear or terror of the physical sort.

She put her other hand on Quution's chest and gave him a look that said *let me*.

He was so rigid he was vibrating, but he tipped his head toward a dark hole in the wall. It wasn't even the typical chamber door, just a busted-out opening in the wall.

Xan crept closer. "Xera," she called in a low voice.

There was no reply.

Her sister was here. She crept closer. "Xera. It's me, Xan."

Like anyone else would be coming for her, but she had to try. Xera might be too terrified to move.

"X-Xan?" Xera's trembling voice drifted out of the dank space.

"Xera!" Xan rushed inside. Spaeth's stench was absent here.

Xera was huddled in the far corner of the chamber. Her eyes weren't wide open and afraid, but shrewd and calculating. Her gaze went past Xan to where Quution hovered outside the door.

Xan raced to Xera's side but scanned the chamber as she did so. It wasn't as small as she'd initially thought. The room was spacious, clean, and opulent by underworld standards. A briny waterfall trickled down the corner opposite where Xera sat.

But there was one thing missing. "Where's Xoda?"

Xan spun in a circle. She didn't sense her niece, and at the moment, she couldn't even recall Xoda's scent.

Xera jumped up. Quution stepped inside like he was going to jump in front of Xan if need be, but it was unnecessary. Xan sent him a small glare. She was grateful for all he'd done, but this was her sister. Xera wouldn't hurt her.

"He has her, Xan." Xera's tinny voice hurt Xan's ears, or perhaps it was the words.

"Where?" Xoda could be anywhere.

"I don't know. If I knew, I'd have gone after her." Her gaze strayed to Quution, but she spoke to Xan. "Did you get what Spaeth wanted?"

The affirmation stuck on Xan's tongue. Xera had been found. They could bring her to safety, but Xoda was in the clutches of the merciless Spaeth.

Though Xera looked hearty.

But demons healed quickly and her kind was adept at mending flesh back together.

Xan glanced at the waterfall again. The chamber wasn't exactly a place of nightmares.

But if Spaeth had brought Xoda to another place to coerce Xera, then he might not spend as much time here. He could just give his orders and leave Xera in fear for her daughter.

Xera's dark gaze met hers. Intense trepidation swelled. Xoda, the precious little girl, was in danger. She was the candy beetle of Xan's eye, the symbol of all that Xan had worked for.

"Yes, I have what Spaeth's after," she said.

"Xan," Quution barked. He inched closer to Xan's side. Xera shrank from him. Xan turned her body to protect Xera from a strange male.

"He's helping us, Xera."

Xera cut a sharp look her way. *"Helping? Why?"*

Shouldn't she be frantic about Xoda, demanding they leave now and search? Finding Xera hadn't been easy, and it'd taken teamwork. But now there was no reason to think they couldn't track down Xoda's location too.

"To put a stop to Spaeth," Xan answered. "Do you know where he's taken her?"

Xera slid her gaze from Quution back to her. "All we have to do is report to Spaeth and he'll free her." She whispered, "Tell me and I'll go free her."

Staggering anxiety almost dropped Xan. She'd do anything to free her niece. She opened her mouth to spill the story, but Quution broke in. "Regardless, we can't talk here. We need to get Xera somewhere safe and cover her trail."

Xera pushed away, shoving Xan back in the process. "He'll be back and I won't be here and then he'll hurt her."

A tremble ran down Xan's spine, but Quution was next to her. His presence calmed her.

"He hasn't summoned Xan yet," he said. "Her time's not up. There's no reason to think he'll be back before he gets his answer from her. We'll find a place for you and when he calls for Xan, we'll be ready for him."

Xera's gaze was hard. Xan didn't expect her to fall into Quution's arms and sigh *my hero*, but the animosity was startling. Then again, this was Xera.

Xan held her hand out. "Come on, Xera. He's right. We can defeat Spaeth and save Xoda. Trust me."

Xera watched her for a heartbeat before accepting her hand. When Xera's cold fingers wrapped around hers, a chill invaded her body, a foreboding. She brushed it off. Xera had been trapped here, alone and terrified.

Xera was safe. Quution and Stryke were on their side. There was no reason to be worried.

AS THEY REVERSED their steps away from Xera's prison, Quution was worried, and it wasn't like before. When Xera had attacked him, the anxiety had been blinding, but not impossible to withstand as long as Xan was on his arm as pictures of her horribly mutilated body flashed through his mind.

Her scent had surrounded him and warded off the worst of the attack. The images flashing through his mind had become more haphazard the closer they'd gotten, as if Xera had been randomly amplifying any fear she could dig up in hopes it'd work.

He didn't like her.

The few minutes they'd been in here, a fretting Xan had soothed Xera while nursing her own terror for the elusive seven- or ten-year-old Xoda. But Xera's attitude had been that of inconvenienced diva rather than out-of-her-mind mother.

Speaking of diva, this was a nice chamber. Personal showers didn't happen in many underworld hovels. Finding a water source that wasn't rank, that wouldn't leave his skin smelling like rotten eggs, was difficult. Either Spaeth was high-maintenance, extremely lucky, or he'd looked long and hard for this spot. And then given it up for Xera.

Would a demon do that for his prisoner?

And Xoda. He couldn't grasp her energy pattern. He knew Xan's individual signature, and now Xera's, but he couldn't sense a third. She'd never been in here, but he'd expect to find some of Xoda's innate energy waves tied to Xera. Nothing.

He walked behind Xan. She had her arm wrapped around her sister. Occasionally, Xera glared over her shoulder at him. Small tendrils of apprehension wound through him, but they were nameless and faceless niggles at his mind that left him antsy and wired.

Xan's shoulders were relaxed. He listened carefully, but she wasn't confessing his plans to Xera. He couldn't afford to leave her alone. He did not trust Xera, and it wasn't because she was a mom shrugging off any attempt to save her kid. It was her eyes. They were cold. Calculating.

His boots scraped the ground, and Xera's annoyed mutters reached him. "Why's he insist on wearing that atrocious clothing? It's noisy and smells."

Okay, one, he didn't smell. He had his own underworld pool to bathe and wash clothing in. Stryke might not say anything about an odor, but Melody wouldn't hesitate, and she usually sighed with relief when he came knocking. *Oh good. You don't smell like a warm, wet carcass.*

And two, how would Xan answer?

"He has his reasons," Xan said. "Don't worry. Quution's not bad."

"You're fucking him." Xera's snide tone raised the hairs on the back of his neck. "I thought you had better taste. He was a target. Mama said never to fuck a target."

"Mama said 'never fuck a target if there's not something in it for you. Don't give your bargaining power away.'" Xan patted Xera's shoulder, and Quution couldn't help but think Xera didn't deserve that comfort. "We'll save Xoda."

Quution strained to hear Xera's next words. "I'd feel better if you told me what you discovered."

"I know, but trust me. It's better this way. Spaeth can't torture you for it."

Xera let out a frustrated growl. "I hate it when you do that. Xoda's going to be the one to pay, not me."

Xan looked over her should at him. Fear churned in her eyes. He gave his head one shake. She scowled, but didn't speak.

He'd have to make sure Xan was never alone with Xera long enough to tell her anything. Because if he let up, she might tell her sister everything. And Xera's best interests were not those of her sister.

CHAPTER 17

*S*tay strong. Quution straightened as much as he dared around Xera. Xan faced him, hands on her hips, eyes flashing. She was gorgeous, and vexed with him.

"How do you think you're going to keep me from staying with my own sister?" she demanded.

"Hear me out," he pleaded.

"I've heard enough."

"Either I stay here with you, or you stay with me next door." Though he was afraid Xera would leave, claiming to look for Xoda.

"Then sit your ass down. I'm not leaving my sister." She turned her back to go to her sister.

Xera sat on a boulder in the middle of the room. They hadn't gone back to his place, or to the library, but found an empty chamber that smelled only of brimstone and dirt. Other beings had left this area alone. He often speculated on the boundaries of the realm. None of his kind had cared to map it, not that they lived long enough to do so. It seemed endless, yet if demons overpopulated it, he had no doubt they

157

would run into each other until fighting and murders culled the herd.

Xan squatted by Xera, who sat more like the Queen of the Nile than a battered abductee. He adjusted his shoulders, that ever-present fidgetiness growing worse. It was Xera. Had to be.

"Are you hungry?" Xan asked her. "When was the last time you ate?"

If she could scare underworld bugs straight to her, she couldn't be that famished. But Xan acted as if she was skin and bones instead of hale and glowing.

Xera looked away in a move that should've come off as fragile, but to Quution it was all artifice. "Spaeth scared off all the food, or by the time they got to me, they were mutated from his radiation."

Xan's energy pulsed over him. Since they'd slept together, he'd become more attuned to her. He could even tell when she was using her ability.

Xera, though… She was outwardly steady, but her energy was not. Was it from suppressed emotion, or was she using her power?

He chose a rock lining the wall and settled on it. Over the next few hours, Xera sent him a glowering look every once in a while, usually when Xan wasn't looking.

Night was approaching, but he could do one full night without sleep. The lack of shut-eye wouldn't diminish his strength too terribly.

His decision was made. He'd watch over Xan and Xera, and depending on what tomorrow brought, he'd have to call in Stryke for help. And for food. He could go longer without food than sleep, and he'd gladly suffer from lack of shut-eye than eat a stinky bug.

Scratches began behind the walls. The females' dinner. He did his own version of meditating while the sisters conversed over their shared meal. Xera eyed him furtively but didn't ask Xan for more dirt on him.

Flaring his energy out, he passed the time like he'd learned to alone in his cell after his mother had died, when he'd read all the books and run out of surface area for his own chicken scratch.

He'd practiced tuning in to the human realm, sifting through energy patterns of vulnerable humans. When he'd come across a source so solid it was uncompromising, he'd studied it. A marvel, a puzzle he'd never been able to work out, but he'd set to weaving his own patterns like theirs. His own armor.

Xan would probably walk right through. Why was that? Demons mated, but they didn't have fated mates. The matings only lasted as long as they were both alive. If one died, the other could mate again. Their rules were much more flexible than those of the vampires, and yet still longer term than human couplings.

He couldn't deny that Xan was no longer the pest of a demon he'd first thought her to be. She'd taken root in the middle of his thoughts. Her upset over warding the under-world made his resolve waver, but it'd keep her safe too—whether she ever forgave him for it or not.

XERA FINALLY DRIFTED off to sleep in the coziest corner of the chamber. Xan could curl up next to her but Xera had never been the touchy-feely type of female. Xoda loved to cuddle.

Memories of her niece had returned in full force. The girl's laughter rang through her head almost every minute, only diminishing when Xera succumbed to sleep.

Poor Xera. Her ribs poked through her skin, her face gaunt. She'd been starved and abused, and she'd lived in constant terror. At least Xan had been able to give her a solid meal.

Xan slipped away, but when she turned around, the only place that would make a decent bed was next to Quution.

She eyed him warily. His presence made it hard for Xera to trust her. She was the only demon Xera could rely on and he was coming between them.

Choosing the rock in the middle of the room that Xera had first sat on, Xan lifted her brow at Quution.

"What do you think?" he asked softly, but his voice still boomed through the room.

She pursed her lips and abandoned her seat. Xera needed safe, uninterrupted rest. Crossing toward Quution, she sank on the floor next to him, but a few feet away.

"I think she's traumatized."

He stared at her, his face unreadable. "Indeed."

The slight patronizing lilt to the word irked her. "Do you think Spaeth was nice? I mean, look at her."

Quution did, then brought his gaze back. "What do you see?"

Xan thrust her hand out and pulled back her shout at the last minute. "Skin and bones. Xera used to be so healthy she glowed."

"She does not have the light purple lines you do."

Xan scowled at him. "We have different sires. I'm so scared for Xoda."

"Mm."

That sound! "You stole that from me."

"It's rather functional. Xan—" He closed his mouth like he'd changed his mind, but then determination filled his eyes. "Do you think it's possible Xera is lying?"

Xan jumped up. "What?"

Xera shifted but remained asleep. Xan pressed her lips together and sat back down.

"I don't see skin and bones." Quution spoke only loud enough for her to hear. "I see a healthy, pampered female."

"We heal quickly."

"Yes, but it's more than her appearance. She doesn't hunch her shoulders. There's no cowering. She can't stand me and she's rude to you. I don't feel that we saved her, but interrupted her."

Xan was shaking her head before she could even process what Quution was saying.

No, no, no. Her sister was not a liar.

"And Xoda—"

Xan went still, her narrowed gaze on Quution. What line of bullshit would come out of his mouth next?

"—how old is she again?"

"What does it matter? She's a kid."

"I can't sense her energy patterns."

"Can you sense Spaeth's?"

Quution tipped his head. "And I could find him if I needed to."

"Well, you've never met Xoda."

"I'd never met Xera but I found her." He twisted to sit facing her. "Xan, demons hide their young well to keep them safe, but there's no hiding from my ability. Xoda's energy should stand out. I don't feel an energy pattern consistent with a child of your kind. I'd expect her energy to be similar to yours and your sister's, but I only sense…you and your sister."

She leaned forward. They were still a few feet apart but close enough to see the earnestness in his features. "Then she's probably farther away. Spaeth might've actually thought outside the box."

"Xan!" Xera cried out.

Xan clambered to Xera's side.

"Lie with me," her sister mumbled.

161

No doubt Quution would point out how Xera's timing was impeccable if given the chance, but it was probably the discussion with Quution that had woken her. And Quution's male voice that had scared her.

"Of course." Xan stretched out beside her to form a barrier against the male behind her. He was trying to get between them, trying to turn her against her only living family member.

She'd have to make sure Quution didn't succeed.

CHAPTER 18

*X*an's eyelids drifted open. A pair of lilac eyes gazed back at her from across the chamber. She'd gone to sleep with her back toward him, like her own personal barrier. A bit of irony since he was obsessed with his wards. But sometime during the night of fretful dreams with a small child's voice crying, "Help me, Auntie Xan," she'd rolled to face Quution.

"I think your sister has finally been sleeping the last couple of hours," he said.

"She's been sleeping all night." Except for the time Xera had woken up and called for her.

He gave his head a slow shake. "No. She was up most of the night and you slept fitfully. You didn't settle down until she drifted off."

Xan sat up, careful not to disturb her sister. "She was asleep the whole night." But her voice didn't ring with the confidence she'd meant it to.

Quution sighed, his face lined with fatigue. "I'm an energy demon, Xan. I can tell when someone is asleep or awake."

"Doesn't mean you'll be truthful about it."

He drew back like she'd physically pushed him. "I don't lie to you."

"Mm." Lying and full disclosure were two different things. She rose to her feet and stretched. His gaze tracked up her body. "I need to grab a bite. Can you stomach a candy beetle?"

She shouldn't offer him food. He didn't like her sister, but somehow she wanted to care for him more than she was leery of him.

"Stryke is bringing food when he comes later."

"Stryke? I don't need another male around my sister. She's been through enough."

His look said *has she?* Xan's lip curled past a fang.

"It's Stryke," he said, not carrying the argument further. "He risked his sanity trying to find her."

She recalled Stryke's time searching the underworld. He hadn't trusted her, but he'd still spent days trying to locate Xera. "Fine, but I'm not leaving her side."

"What about when Spaeth summons you?"

"I'll leave to kill him." She wasn't playing anymore. Xoda could still be found with Spaeth dead.

"I will be by your side."

Her anger at Quution was swept away by other feelings. Desire. Compassion. And a deeper emotion she didn't care to look at too closely right now. The last several hours, she'd been nothing but bitchy and suspicious.

It was the turmoil of the time. Xoda was missing. Xera was recovering. Quution was saying outlandish things. Had to be the aftereffects of Xera's influence on him. Xera had been going full power, frantic to stay hidden to protect Xoda.

Xoda and her tinkling laugh. Xan cocked her head. She couldn't hear Xoda's laughter right now. Yet only hours ago, she couldn't get it out of her mind.

How old was Xoda anyway?

No, it didn't matter. She wasn't going to agonize over details that wouldn't save the girl's life.

She abandoned talking to Quution, using the excuse that she needed to lure food when really, looking at him hurt. He was back in his grungy threads and prosthetics and she still drooled when she looked at him. His keen eyes, those full lips, and that hair she loved sinking her hands in when he—

Guess looking at him wasn't the problem. She had to think about something else. Concentrating on the walls, she fooled the beetles into thinking Spaeth was chasing them. She snatched the first candy beetle to emerge and popped it into her mouth. Sweetness exploded over her tongue. She'd offer one to Quution, but the shade of green he'd turned when she and Xera had eaten the previous day hadn't gone unnoticed.

There was nothing wrong with eating like she was raised to do. It's not like they could have a cattle ranch in the underworld. Or grow carrots. Mill their own grains. Erect a chocolate factory. They were the prey or the predators and in most cases they were both.

She couldn't summon enough righteousness to stay irritated with him. His formative years hadn't been kind, but most of their kind was raised that way. Yet Quution wasn't like the rest of them. He'd gotten smart instead of vicious, and it showed in how he cared deeply for those close to him.

Just wait. Once he got to know Xera, once she healed, his opinion of her would change.

Xan glanced at the sleeping form of her sister. She was looking better already. Yesterday, Xan had been ready to mainline candy beetles straight into her to build some meat back on her bones. This morning, the urgency was gone. Xera's hips were rounded, her face filled out, and her muscles defined.

Where Xan was darker shades of purple with lighter

lines, Xera was like an exotic orchid, the underworld's very own flower with shades of violet and indigo interspersed with more pink-hued purples, like fuchsia. Xoda's colorings were similar. She could practically be her mother's twin from that age.

She polished off a third candy beetle before turning back to Quution. He was brooding quietly on his rock. She'd ask what he was thinking about, but unless it was about finding Xoda, Xan didn't care. He was so set on imprisoning them down here, she'd have to reconcile her life to the underworld to protect Xera and Xoda.

Footsteps crunched. Xan spun to the entrance. More than one being was out there. Who had found them?

Quution wasn't concerned. He raised his gaze to hers, then to the door. Stryke entered first. As he shrewdly took in the scene, tracking the tension between her and Quution and a sleeping Xera, a female entered behind him.

Stryke was wearing black pants, a black long-sleeved shirt, and boots—also black, not that Xan cared if he was naked or encased in overalls. But the female wasn't a demon. Xan sniffed. A definite lack of brimstone, but not the distinct sense of fragility humans threw off.

Vampire. Was this his mate, Zoey? Her brown hair was wrapped in a severe bun and she wore clothing similar to Stryke's. Xan's lips twitched. Yes. Stryke's mate. He'd used his energy to keep her dressed between realms.

Quution rose, looking ready to shuffle away despite sitting on that damn rock for hours. Did nothing come hard to him?

Zoey spoke, keeping her volume down as her eyes bounced off her and Xera. "I tagged along so Stryke wouldn't have to leave every ten minutes to check on me."

Xan's defenses rose. "Xera will no longer be trying to keep Stryke from finding her. She is safe with us."

Stryke's gaze darted to Quution's and an unspoken exchange passed between them. Xan clenched her teeth against the wave of jealousy that coursed through her. She and Xera had never had that type of connection. With the way Xera had been raised, Xan was more like the disciplinarian mama that Xera should've had in the first place.

Zoey pinned her with a hard but curious gaze. "You are Xan?"

"The one and only," Xan answered, not yet sure she liked Zoey.

For a vampire, the female was all sorts of no-nonsense. In Xan's limited experience with vampires, they were usually vain and coy, but Zoey had a confident and practical air about her. She wasn't flustered at being in the same room as two purple demons, and there was no air of superiority.

"No summons yet?" Stryke asked. He handed over a fast food bag that emanated savory smells.

Quution shook his head as he dug into the bag. He retrieved something cylindrical and foil wrapped. A breakfast burrito?

Xan's preference for sweets carried into the human realm too. She was a pancakes-and-syrup girl. Marcus probably added two extra workouts each week after she splurged on breakfast when she was in charge of him.

Quution carefully peeled away a wrapper to keep his claws from catching. "We should come up with a plan."

His gaze strayed to Xera. Stryke's did the same. Then they exchanged another look. Stryke's nod was nearly imperceptible.

The brothers were up to something, and they weren't telling her about it. Reality crashed into Xan. She was going to have to choose between Xera and Quution.

And the decision was harder than she'd ever thought it would be.

~

QUUTION RIPPED off a hunk of burrito and popped it into his mouth. It was the only way he could eat without smearing his food all over his chin to drip down his fake fangs.

Watching Xan eat her candy beetles had almost gotten him to change his mind about waiting for food. She savored her sweets, even if they were in the form of disgusting underworld beetles. Her eyes would close and bliss would cross her face and he wanted to hunt every candy beetle in the realm and hand-feed them to her.

From the rigid set of her shoulders and the hooded glares she sent him and Stryke, she'd probably toss the beetles back in his face.

He did not trust Xera. But until he knew more, he'd keep his hunches to himself. And between him and Stryke, who had probably passed their convictions along to Zoey, which was why she was here.

Xera was good. Whatever she was up to, she had Xan fooled, though she was probably the only being alive who could get to Xan. Did she have her own plan? Xera likely knew that Xan had been sent to spy on him. So was she planning on using that info to her own advantage? Or had she teamed up with Spaeth?

Stryke crossed to stand next to him. It would be hard to hide their conversation in the chamber, but that wasn't the goal. Xera was awake and she was listening.

"Are you going with Xan when she meets with Spaeth?" Stryke asked.

"Yes."

"Think you can take him?"

"Absolutely." Quution attuned himself to Xera and the energy she expended breathing and the noticeable increase of her heart rate. She was awake and if she was awake, she had to be listening. So was Xan. The females wouldn't let the opportunity pass. Didn't mean Xera wasn't plotting. She hadn't let anyone know she'd awakened for a reason.

What was she up to?

As for whether Quution could fight Spaeth, he wasn't as certain as he'd made it sound. Spaeth was his own form of energy demon. He couldn't manipulate others' energies, but he was an expert in wielding his own. Quution could sense him, but he was just as susceptible to Spaeth's powers as any other demon. Healing while fighting Spaeth would drain him as much as the battle.

Plus, he had Xan to worry about. The thought of that full-breed searing a millimeter of her skin made his energy sizzle. Quution was certain she could defend herself in hand-to-hand combat—but that was where Spaeth had one up on them. It was hard to grapple with a demon long enough to pin him when one's skin was blistering off.

Then there was Xera. Would the meeting with Spaeth be a trap? If she was working with him, then when Quution left with Xan, his brother and Zoey would be at risk. Each of them might think they were safe from Xera's powers since they were together, but Xan also thought she saw a female that was starving and beaten, not sullen and manipulative.

Quution had to get a rise out of her. He couldn't walk into a confrontation with Xan and have Xera be an unknown.

"Too bad Spaeth doesn't summon Xan now," he said to Stryke. "Then we could leave before Xera wakes."

Stryke glanced at Xera and then at Zoey. "She wouldn't have to worry about the kid."

Zoey's lips pursed. Good. Stryke had filled her in on their concerns regarding "the kid."

Xan started pacing. He waited for her glare but it never came. She avoided eye contact, her concentration centered on the floor. A glimpse of white from her fang peeked out as she chewed at her lower lip with the tip.

Those fangs that had nipped his skin only yesterday. And now she wouldn't even look at him.

Something was wrong.

"Xan." He started for her, but froze.

In front of him, a nightmare played across his vision. Spaeth appeared in front of Xan, red glowing from his eyes and under his skin. Her body went taut and she threw her head back to cry out. The burning. The stench. Xan was being fried alive.

"No!" Quution ran to save Xan, only to smack face-first into the wall, his head banging off. He stumbled, but his only thought was that he'd failed. Xan had perished.

CHAPTER 19

*W*hat the ever-loving hell had gotten into Quution? A brush of wind caressed her skin as he rushed past her and body slammed the wall.

Dirt shuffled as Xera jumped up and grabbed her hand. "Come on," she yelled and pulled Xan behind her.

Quution was ignoring the danger to Xoda and planned to save only himself. Quution was going to pit her against her sister and Xoda would suffer, and—

Wait, what was going on?

Xan stared around her, her feet stumbling one after the other as Xera dragged her. It was like slow motion. Quution staggering back, trying to stay on his feet. The cry of anguish ripping from his chest calling to her on a primal level. He was hurting.

Stryke sprinted to Quution's side. Zoey spun to charge after her. Xan's power lashed out without finesse. The couple had thought being together would make it easier to stand against a demon like her sister. But a mated couple was the easiest target of all: the other always their greatest weakness.

Xan cast the impression that Quution was attacking Stryke in his mindless despair. She sent Zoey an image of those garish, long claws sinking into Stryke's chest. Zoey's face paled and she spun toward the males.

It would have to be enough.

"I can keep up the hallucination on the ugly one," Xera said. "Can you take care of that disgusting couple?"

Stryke and Zoey could be July in a hot-couples-of-the-underworld calendar. But Xera scorned anyone she thought was lesser than her and that was usually everyone. Not to mention, she didn't know Quution's true appearance.

"I've got them," Xan said with conviction. She switched back and forth so quickly, the hallucination wouldn't have time to fade. As she and her sister put more distance between them and the other three, it would get harder. She and Xera would have to cast a net much like Xera had done when they'd been looking for her.

Guilt gnawed at her, the sense of wrongness disturbing. But she had to get away, to find Xoda before Spaeth could turn her niece against them. Quution was going to remove her from the Circle and put Stryke on it. Then, underworld domination. Or something like that.

Xan blinked. Quution wasn't the domination type. How had she not seen that coming?

He was still a demon.

What had made him so frantic back there? She'd spent days with him, months lurking around him, and she hadn't sensed a fear that would make him run headlong into a wall.

They were sprinting through the corridors. After one turn, they happened upon three half-breeds lingering in the halls like school kids who didn't want to report to class. Their jaundiced gazes landed on Xan and Xera and there were three smiles full of sharp teeth. Xan couldn't determine if they were male or female; they were barely humanoid.

She couldn't release her illusions to fight these beasts. They'd have to do it the old-fashioned way. Neither she nor Xera slowed. They rammed into the demons, elbows, feet, and claws flying.

The half-breeds didn't have a chance against them. Xera was as ruthless a fighter as Xan. A wet splatter and a shriek of agony bounced off the walls. Xera's malicious laugh drowned out the cries as she beat one demon with its own arm.

Okay, so Xera was *more* ruthless a fighter.

The three demons down and twitching, they continued their sprint.

"Overkill?" Xan huffed. Xera favored the easy route and that usually equated to violence in her mind.

The effort of maintaining a strong hallucination over a longer distance while running and fighting was draining her. She eased up. Both Zoey and Stryke would know the other was okay, but they'd be dogged by horrible premonitions and have to keep checking their mate's status. And who knew what Xera was doing to Quution.

Xan's jaw tightened. She couldn't count how many times during their flight she'd wanted to tell Xera to stop. Knock it off and leave Quution alone. He'd been sporting a broken nose and a concussion before they'd even left the chamber.

Xan was about to fly around a corner when Xera yanked her arm the other direction.

"This way."

A twinge pinged in Xan's ankle as she pivoted to follow Xera.

Her sister's pace slowed to a speed walk. Her shoulders hung and her sides heaved. Xan wasn't as worn out and used the opportunity to scan her surroundings.

She wasn't familiar with this part of the underworld,

which meant little, given the vastness of the realm. But Xera seemed to know where she was going.

"Do you have a hiding place in mind?" Xan asked.

Xera shot her a hard look. "Hide? Don't we have to save the kid? You need to tell Spaeth everything."

What was with everyone calling Xoda "the kid"? She had a name.

Xan tripped over her own feet, like a thought was pushing so hard to get out, it was interfering with her stride.

The image of Xera beating the strange demon with its own limb ran through her mind. The act didn't bother her as much as the gleeful smile on Xera's face. It had been like witnessing the flower of the underworld turn into a six-foot Venus flytrap. Times like those made Xan worry she hadn't offset Mama's evil influence as much as she'd hoped.

But Xera had saved her. Quution had plotted against her and she'd stopped him with only a thought. Xera had channeled and manipulated his fear better than Xan ever had, though Xan had gone for subtlety, a tactic she'd worked hard with Xera to master.

"What did you make Quution think was happening?" Xan couldn't admit that she'd never been that successful with him. Her attraction must've gotten in the way.

"That Spaeth was killing you."

Xan snorted. "No, really." She'd never detected herself as Quution's weakness, and she'd had him inside her.

"Why would you think I was lying?" Xera ran her tongue along her teeth. "I'd been dying to make him see that, to tease him with your slow death. I hated pretending to be asleep while he chitchatted with his vile brother."

Xan drew in a sharp breath. "But I'm not his weakness."

She'd been in his fantasy, but only because he'd wanted to fuck her. It wasn't like he had a lot of options down here. She was the only female who knew that he was a half-breed, and she was bound by their bargain to keep his secret. Except, there were plenty of ways he could fuck someone without revealing his true identity. She'd almost taken him in the chair, fully clothed.

None of that mattered when he planned to leave forever. To leave *her* forever. How much could she mean to him?

Xera rolled her eyes. "Yes, most guys ram their heads into a wall because the female they absolutely don't care about is burning alive. He was trying to save you. *You're welcome.*" She growled. "*You* might sense only fear, but I'm still stronger with it."

Someone had woken up on the wrong side of the dirt floor. Xera had always gloated about her power and Xan had never argued. Instead, she'd doubled down on teaching Xera compassion and cunning instead of brute force. There was a time and place for each tactic, but to Xera, it was always time for a fight. Who could best who in the fear department hadn't been a concern of Xan's.

Xera was better at being an empath. That must be why she'd sensed Quution's vulnerability when it'd come to Xan. Had her own connection with him interfered? The only time her kind was oblivious to a weak point was when they were reading their—

Xan's heart slammed against her ribs. She put a hand to her chest.

No. Her kind didn't do love. Talk about setting themselves up for failure. They resisted attachments and didn't mate.

Sure, she prided herself in being an unconventional demon, but this was just…ridiculous.

And if Quution was so damn worried about her, why was he wedging himself between her and Xera? He was turning on her.

Xan's continued silence must've inspired Xera's irritated

hiss. "Mama was wrong. I could still beat you no matter how well you mastered fear."

Mama had said she was the strong one? "She was trying to make you jealous."

Xera sucked her teeth, the smacking sound echoing off the walls.

Xan frowned and watched the floor as she walked. How was Quution turning on her again?

She looked at Xera from under her lashes. Her sister's lips were curved in her typical perma-sneer. She was catching her breath, but tension radiated from her.

Quution didn't trust her sister.

I'm an energy demon, Xan. I can tell when someone is asleep or awake.

Xera had been awake, listening to the brothers talk about going to Spaeth and killing him. When exactly had Quution plotted against her?

Xan's steps slowed.

Quution didn't trust her sister, and Xan trusted Quution.

The realization startled her. She'd never trusted anyone other than Xera, and truthfully, she'd always had doubts. But only because Xera was brash, impulsive, and so damn resentful. But Xan trusted Quution.

If she were to evaluate her own weaknesses, she'd find three. Xera, Xoda, and Quution.

How old is Xoda?

Quution had asked her that more than once. Maybe it was time she found out.

"Xera, how old is Xoda?"

Xera slanted a dark look her way but kept walking. Her pace kicked up.

"Xera!" Xan barked.

"What does it matter? It's not like we're planning a birthday party soon."

Xan had inhabited enough humans to know that kids' ages were a fact mothers didn't have to think about. Sure, there were the times they were harried, their minds churning with a million different details—like being possessed by a demon, for one—but they could rattle off their kids' ages and birthdays without fail.

"Why can't you answer?"

Xera cut her hand through the air. "Because I'm worried. My daughter has been kidnapped and you're asking inane questions."

Familiar anxiety churned Xan's stomach, anxiety that hadn't been there minutes ago.

"Where are we going?" Xan slowed as Xera sped up.

Xera threw a glare over her shoulder and stopped when she saw how far back Xan had gotten. "You're wasting time. They're after us."

Facts. Details. They were fear's biggest weakness. Xan took a fortifying breath. "Spaeth wants to know what Quution's up to. He kidnapped—" Xan briefly shut her eyes. Facts. "He said he kidnapped you and Xoda to get me to work for him." The reverse wouldn't have worked. He couldn't have abducted Xan to coerce Xera into cooperating because Xera would have just let Xan languish.

The knowledge cracked her heart.

"We already know this." Xera huffed. "Why are you wasting time?"

"You kept us away from you, saying it was for Xoda's safety. Yet every time Quution asks me how old she is, I have no answer. And each time I think of her, she looks exactly like you when you were younger. *Exactly* like you."

No two demons were alike.

Instead of asking, Xan said it. "She's not real."

Xera bared her fangs. "You wanted to save me so badly. Your love was ripe for the picking." She shrugged. "I needed you off my back. So I gave you a kid to save. You always said I wasn't patient enough. How was that? I started her as a baby, knowing one day, I could use her against you."

Xan's heart splintered in two. Her niece wasn't real.

A sob tore from her throat.

Xera's evil laugh didn't belong to the sister Xan had thought she'd known. "Who's the strong sister now?" She tossed her head back. "If only Mama could see you now. You know, I should've known she was toying with my insecurities like a proper mama would." A snide look crossed her face. "But then I wouldn't know, would I? I've never been a mama."

The battle cry ripping from Xan's throat was as unexpected as it was powerful. She launched herself at Xera.

Her claws met skin and she curled them in, digging as deep as possible. Xera screeched and tried to wrench herself away, leaving several gashes in the process.

Xan kneed and kicked. Xera threw a punch at her face, but Xan flashed her fangs, shredding her sister's hand.

"You bitch!" Xera stomped on her foot.

This wasn't a cold and calculated fight. It was decades of Xera's resentment and all of Xan's broken heart.

Xoda wasn't real. Xan hadn't saved her sister, and the niece she adored had never existed. She poured her fury at herself into the battle as they clawed and bit each other. Xan had been clueless, had refused to notice that Xoda's memory was only strong around her sister. She'd been chasing the idea of family, too influenced by her time in the human realm to realize that notion didn't exist in demons.

Xan snaked an arm around Xera's neck and tightened her into a headlock. "Are you working for Spaeth?"

"He's working for me," she hissed and elbowed her in the side.

"Am I?" a male's voice purred next to their ear.

Xan gasped at the searing pain on the side of her face and released Xera.

"She knows," Xera shouted.

Spaeth fully formed beside Xan.

Shit. She couldn't back up fast enough to avoid the inferno licking over her skin.

Tingles coursed over the pain and a bolt of light shot over her shoulder to nail Spaeth in the side.

"What the—" Xan was grateful for the reprieve.

The three of them whipped their heads in the direction of the attack. Quution's hand was poised to lob another.

Spaeth hissed, steam streaming out of his mouth. He clamped a hand on Xera and her mouth dropped open in pain. They both disappeared, her sister's gasp lingering in the air.

Xan sagged, her hands going to her knees, blood tracing rivulets down her skin and dripping onto the floor. "She's not… She's not…real."

A long, mournful cry resonated from her chest. She met Quution's sympathetic stare. He'd known. Or at least had suspected. He'd tried to help her see the truth.

Maybe he did know what was best for the realm.

She slammed her eyes shut. Before her next breath, she disappeared.

QUUTION HAD ROUNDED the corner moments before Spaeth appeared, Stryke and Zoey on his heels. The two sisters were too busy fighting to notice their arrival, much less Spaeth's. But before Quution could dive into the fray, Spaeth had snatched Xera, and now Xan was just…gone. He caught his breath as he took in the scene of the scuffle before him.

In the other chamber, Xan had aided her sister's escape.

The knockdown, drag-out fight he'd come upon had been unexpected, to say the least. The pain in her eyes had had nothing to do with her own injuries. She'd fought with her sister, but she hadn't been hurt physically as much as mentally.

She's not...real.

Xera had created an entire person to fool Xan. His female's repayment for caring for her family was total heartbreak.

"I have to find her." It wasn't a mystery where she'd gone. He glanced at Zoey and bowed his head. "Thank you for your help."

Zoey shook her head. "I wasn't a big help. How can you be sure this isn't an elaborate ruse to split us up?"

"Because..." The answer didn't come. He just knew. Xera had been the one to make the first move toward escape, and he'd already had reason to think she was using her powers on her sister. Xan had gone along with the escape plan, but *she* hadn't run him into a wall, nor had she hurt Stryke or Zoey. She pumped massive amounts of fear for each other into them, yes. But if she and Xera had been working together, she would've had time to twist Stryke and Zoey against each other. Quution didn't have to have Xan's abilities to know that Stryke's worst fear was not just that Zoey would get hurt, but that he'd be the cause.

"Quution," Stryke prodded when he didn't continue. "Find her. We will wait to search for Spaeth until you return." Stryke's gaze strayed to the last spot Xera had been in. "Since there's no little girl in danger."

Zoey shook her head. "I didn't think I'd ever feel sorry for someone like Xan, but damn...that's harsh."

Quution nodded. "Unconscionable."

He searched for the familiar energy pattern of future-college-grad Brooklyn. She was there, still uneasy about what to expect when she was officially kicked out of the nest, still a ripe host for him to slide into.

She stiffened as he muscled her consciousness out of the way but then relaxed like she was grateful for the mental reprieve, happy to not have to stress for a few minutes. He shook his head, her blond hair flying. So much worry for such a young human. Weren't they supposed to be dancing with glee at the chance to carve out a life of their own?

Quution blinked, adjusting to the body. A laptop was open in front of him and he sat on a couch in an economy apartment that had seen better days thirty years ago. This… was not the place he'd expected his host to live. Her car probably cost more than this entire building.

But that was a worry for another day. He had to find Xan. Checking to see if he had to save anything before he closed the laptop, he flipped through the various sites she had open. Job postings and descriptions littered the page.

No wonder Brooklyn's anxiety was giving her heartburn. He rubbed his chest. The discomfort didn't ease and he set the laptop down. After locating keys, he charged out the door.

Would Xan be at Marcus's? She'd be in Marcus, but where would he be? It was the middle of the day, and Quution didn't often track the days of the week humans lived by, but he didn't think it was the weekend. Xan had mentioned that Marcus worked from home.

The drive went quickly despite sticking to the speed limit even though he wanted to stomp on the gas and fly through town.

What did Marcus drive? Quution parked in front of Marcus's building and ran to the foyer door. It was locked.

With a frustrated growl that would've bared his own fangs, but only showed Brooklyn's even white teeth, he spun around, trying to figure out what to do next.

Muted thumps sounded behind him and he turned back to the door. A tall man about the same age as Brooklyn banged the door open, a smile lighting his face when his gaze landed on Quution's host.

"Hey. Haven't seen you around here before." He held the door open and Quution skirted around him to get inside, keeping his eyes down. Brooklyn's eyes would be ink black, and startled humans did stupid things.

"I'm looking for Marcus." The human had already proved useful; perhaps he was full of answers.

"Nice." The way the guy said it, Quution wasn't sure if he should preen or pepper spray the man. "He's probably at the gym."

Damn. He'd planned to sprint up the stairs and pound on Marcus's door until she let him in or went back to the underworld, but Xan wasn't going to come back here if Marcus was already out. She'd know that Quution would check here first.

"Oh." He needed the helpful man to provide more details. "That one down on…"

"Third and Piedmont, yeah." The man reclined against the doorframe, blocking Quution's exit as he eyed the trim body of the host. "But I can entertain you until he gets back."

The man needed to move and Quution couldn't face him to tell him off. Accessing his powers mid possession was like dragging an anchor through deep waters, but he managed to send a jolt of electricity through the steel doorframe.

The guy yelped and stumbled out the door. Quution breezed past him. "Thanks for the help." The stranger was too busy rubbing his shoulder and inspecting the doorframe to respond before Quution was back in the car and peeling out of the lot.

CHAPTER 20

*A*n unfamiliar voice filtered through the stall door. "Uh…you, like, okay in there, dude?"

Marcus's shoulders shook as sobs racked his body. Xan had tried to hold it together. She'd appeared in Marcus, dropped the fifty-pound kettlebell, and marched to the locker room. She'd only meant to grab keys and get the hell out of there. All she had to do was make it to his car before she lost her shit.

But shit had gotten lost once she'd reached the quiet of the locker room. The crying had started and she couldn't stop. Now she was perched on a toilet in a long line of stalls, sniffling and sobbing in Marcus's deep keen.

"F-fine," she managed to get out.

"Uh-huh," the guy replied, but his feet disappeared from the other side of the door.

Unrolling a wad of toilet paper, she blew her nose and wiped her eyes. Marcus was going to feel like a train wreck when she was done with him, but she didn't plan on leaving him anytime soon.

Was she strong enough to permanently possess a host?

There was no way she was going back to the underworld. What kind of being would fake a fucking kid being born— and then carry on the lie for years?

Her crazy sister.

How long had Xera been an evil bitch? Had she ever had a chance at being decent, or had Mama robbed all innocence from her? Or had Xera been born wicked and preferred to stay that way?

Xan rose and brushed herself off. Tossing the tissue into the toilet, she flushed and left. The locker room was empty once again.

In the mirror, Marcus's face looked ashen and haggard. He'd probably been like that before she possessed him today. His body was sluggish, and walking was like trudging through molten iron. He was working out too much again.

Food. That was on her agenda for the day. Food and rest. Marcus was so worn out that his consciousness wasn't even fighting her.

No protein-rich diet today, big guy. She was going to the ice cream shop next door and picking up a gallon. Maybe two. And a spoon, no bowls necessary. Then she'd fill the gas tank and drive to a park where she could drown her sorrows in cold, creamy guilt.

Not bothering to change out of the workout basketball shorts and tight black tee, she grabbed Marcus's keys and wallet and kept her head down, walking through the hall to the front office.

A vaguely recognizable voice was arguing with the front desk clerk. "I just need to see if he's here." The high-pitched tone didn't bother her as much as it should.

"I'm sorry, but only members are allowed inside." The clerk was standing her ground against a petite, curvy blond.

Wait…Xan knew those highlights.

184

"Quution?" The clerk's brow scrunched and Xan realized her error. "Um, Brooklyn?"

The girl spun around, her pristine hair twirling. She wore sunglasses and lowered them to peer at her. Solid black eyes peered over the rim. "Good."

Quution sounded so relieved, Xan wanted to roll in the feeling of his concern. She'd been his worst nightmare—the fear of her getting hurt. But she'd also psychically attacked his brother and Zoey trying to get away. She'd left Quution at her sister's lack of mercy.

The tiny blonde grabbed his elbow and towed him out, not giving the clerk a backward glance. "You need to hide your eyes."

"They're not exactly my priority. That front desk girl ignores me half the time."

Outside, she blinked in the sun, wishing Marcus were wearing his shades after all. "How did you find me?"

"Unlike the human here, there was an overly helpful man at your apartment building."

"Digger." The name came so instantly, she triple-checked her hold over Marcus. Curiosity was the only emotion she sensed from the man. She could do that for him, at least. Take his mind off his own troubles and let him see how much worse they could be.

"Whatever the man's name, he told me where you'd be."

"Why are you here? I'm not going back to the underworld so you can imprison me."

Quution stopped, his pert little face scrunched up. He was offended. "I'm not going to imprison you. Why would you think…"

She lifted a dark brow. When hadn't he imprisoned her?

"Point made. I'm not going to lock you away. I know what Xera did to you."

For a few brief minutes, her mind had been off her sister

and her grief over Xoda. But it all slammed back into her. Her eyes burned with tears and she inhaled a shaky breath. "I had no idea."

"We often think the best of family, even when they're the worst."

She sob-snorted. "Not your most elegant insight. But you're right. Xera is the worst."

He nodded. "As were our parents. They had the worst role models and an atrocious environment. It doesn't excuse their behavior, but I hope it tells you that the fault is not yours."

"I'm a demon. I should've known better."

He lifted a tiny shoulder. Xan didn't covet Brooklyn's diminutive size, but she was shapely. And hostility no longer plagued her since Brooklyn didn't cut it in Quution's fantasies. "We're half-breeds, and sometimes we forget the other half that's not demonic. When it comes to nature versus nurture, some of us embraced our full natures better than others."

But none of his words made her feel better. The image of her non-niece was already fading. "She wasn't real. Do you know how fucked up that is?"

Quution tightened his grip and towed her toward Brooklyn's car. "Let's go back to your place and talk."

"We need to stop for food first. Marcus is hurting himself again, only he does it by being über healthy. I doubt there's anything at his place but protein powder and chicken breasts."

Quution opened his pink, glossed lips, then shut them again. Xan knew him well enough by now to know that he'd been about to censure her.

"Maybe if I get some carbs into him, he won't feel like he's dragging his ass through every workout. He's so lean he's losing muscle mass." Xan wanted a healthy host, not an anorexic over-exerciser. But Marcus probably didn't have a brother who had faked parenthood.

"There is an ice cream place across the road. Do you know if Marcus has sunglasses in his car?"

"They have a drive-through. Leave his car here." If Quution wasn't going to drag her back to the underworld, then she was going to hide in Marcus's apartment and lick her wounds.

Quution drove Brooklyn's sedan to the shop, not saying anything as she rattled off her order and then headed for Marcus's apartment after they got her stash. "I'd take you back to Brooklyn's, but I think you'd make the minuscule place feel cramped." He chattered about Brooklyn's job hunt all the way, like he knew Xan was comforted by the everyday life and struggles of humans.

How was she supposed to survive her own life in the underworld? There was no pleasure to be found. No thirty flavors of ice cream to choose from or bright sunshine to chase away the shadows, and no apartments she could lock herself in. In her realm, she had to be *on* all the time. Be at the ready or risk being killed in a horrible way that would make her wish for death.

She'd let her guard down around the one person she'd thought she could trust and look what had happened.

"I wish I could live here."

Quution swung into a parking spot. "I wish you could, too."

"I won't even be able to visit." Xan didn't want to delve into an argument, but she couldn't miss the opportunity to point out the obvious.

"This isn't a life meant for demons," he said gently.

Damn him, it was true. Either Marcus would figure out a way to boost her out of him, or he'd eventually pass away. She couldn't find another host on her own.

She got out and led Quution inside. Fumbling with the keys, she unlocked the door and held it for him. His arms were laden with her solace for the next few hours.

Once inside Marcus's apartment, she dropped the keys and went straight for the kitchen. She located the spoons, grabbed two, and plopped on the couch.

Quution stood on the welcome mat, athletic shoes toed off and lined up neatly at the edge.

She ran her tongue along Marcus's even teeth. "If you're going to stand there and watch, hand over the tub of tin roof. And the jar of hot fudge."

Quution glanced toward the kitchen, probably wondering why she hadn't gotten a bowl or two, then at his armload. He tossed her the bin of tin roof sundae and went to the kitchen.

Whatever, she didn't need hot fudge anyway. Popping the lid, she dug in. The microwave whirred in the kitchen, followed by a ding. Quution reemerged with the jar.

She'd made enough of a dent for him to pour some of the jar inside the ice cream tub.

"Sweet," she said, and tackled that section.

He selected the other spoon and joined her. They ate in silence. Was his stomach feeling a little queasy like hers? Marcus hadn't been ready for several hundred calories of fat and sugar and his gut was complaining.

"Uh," she said, pushing up. "I need some water. You?"

"Please." Quution put his spoon down. He'd just been eating with her so she wasn't alone.

Hot tears welled in her eyes. She blinked them back as she filled her glass. Chugging it, she took a moment to center herself.

Much better.

But Quution was behind her, stuffing the ice cream in the freezer.

"What the hell?" She glared at where he'd tossed the utensils into the sink. "I wasn't done."

"You're not eating until you make yourself sick."

"Fine. I'll have it for breakfast."

Quution's soft sigh was obnoxiously loud in the quiet apartment. "Xan. Talk to me."

She slammed a hand on her hip. "About what? How shitty I feel? How I'm grieving for a kid who never existed? How mad I am at myself for not seeing through my sister?"

"Yes."

"It won't do any good."

"Neither will hiding in Marcus."

Xan rubbed her suddenly pounding temples. Now she was angry at Quution for being right about eating until Marcus was on the floor and heaving. "I'm going to take a nap."

It was midday. She just wanted oblivion.

She crawled into Marcus's king-sized bed. A tug at her feet made her look up. Quution was taking her shoes off. Since she'd flopped on top of the bedding, he grabbed a neatly folded quilt and draped it over her.

She blinked, staring at the far wall, ignoring Quution and his attempts to make her more comfortable. Her mouth tasted sour, her stomach was as heavy as the kettlebell Marcus had used earlier, and she was tired. So damn tired.

The bed dipped under the diminutive weight of Brooklyn's body. Quution snuggled behind her. His host was small but solid against her back.

Tears streaked down her cheeks until her blinks grew longer and she finally succumbed to sleep.

QUUTION HAD NEVER FELT SO powerless in his life. Xan was

understandably depressed, but she wasn't crawling out of it. She'd been in Marcus for two days and he sensed the human had withdrawn so far that Xan could take over his body for another decade.

He missed Xan's lively chats, her zest for learning, and the way she used to vex him so—on purpose.

This Xan was despondent. She wouldn't even eat any more ice cream. When was the last time she'd moved off the couch? She watched true crime documentaries. Horrible, depressing stories that fit better in his realm than the human one.

Quution had showered, but all he'd had were Brooklyn's yoga pants and oversize T-shirt. The bra had had to go. It was folded neatly on top of Brooklyn's shoes. Her constant worry over applying for jobs ate at him until he'd booted up Marcus's computer and applied for her. There was nothing else to do, so he kept up the job search. His host had mellowed, oddly at peace with his interference.

Fabric rustled and the couch creaked. Quution glanced up, hopeful she was finally rising to take a piss, or get a drink, but no. She had flopped onto her back, a large foot hanging off one armrest. Unlike him, she hadn't showered. Stains from the first day's melted ice cream dotted her black shirt. When he'd mentioned an outfit change at the very least, she'd told him he was free to leave.

He'd stayed.

A knock pounded on the door.

He tensed, coiling a lash of energy to be at the ready. Xan did nothing but cock a brow at him and return to her show. This one was about a woman killing her sister because she'd been having an affair with her brother-in-law and wanted him for herself. Quution had better survival skills than to suggest she find a new channel.

Should he answer the door?

"Q, it's me." Stryke.

Quution didn't move for the door. Would Stryke's presence help or hurt Xan's recovery? Regardless, he was grateful Stryke had given him some time with Xan before tracking him down.

If she reacted to Stryke's announcement, she didn't show it, her dull gaze on the TV.

"Just a minute," Quution called just so Stryke wouldn't pound on the door again. Or maybe he should take his time and see if the ruckus roused Xan. He had a feeling it wouldn't.

Flipping the deadbolt, he opened to Stryke. As always, a quick shot of jealousy speared him. Stryke was mated to Zoey and could roam the realm in his own form. He had a ball cap pulled down over his horns with sunglasses resting on the brim to hide his unique eye color when needed.

Stryke didn't bat an eye at his host. He wasn't interested in the woman and he was accustomed to a new host each time they met up. But when he stepped in and spotted Xan on the couch, a brow crept up. Quution closed and relocked the door.

"Hey," was all Xan said.

To prevent talking about Xan like she wasn't there, Quution suggested, "Perhaps we should step into the office."

"I can take whatever you have to say." Xan curled onto her side. Her shirt rode up, exposing a dark swath of skin and toned abs. "I don't care anyway."

"So that's how it is." Stryke didn't bother to take his shoes off. He retrieved a chair from the kitchen table and straddled it so he could rest his arms across the back. "Because Xera and Spaeth aren't wasting time. Melody said they know you're both gone and they've been telling the rest of the Circle that you're working together to take over the realm or whatever. Treason. It doesn't take much to rile up a bunch of mindless beasts."

Quution grunted. "As if the rest of them aren't planning their own takeover."

Xan spoke up, her voice hard. "Why do you even care? It's not like you're staying down there."

An outcome he'd once anticipated, but now the thought of leaving for eternity wasn't so welcome. He switched his attention to Stryke's news. "It's only been a couple of days. It'll take months to sway the other ten members of the Circle against us." Melody would never fall for it.

Stryke shook his head. "Not with Xera's help. I swear she put the literal fear of God into them. Creed has all but begged Melody to stop going down there at all. Both he and I are accompanying her."

Sweet brimstone. Why hadn't he considered that Xera had partnered with Spaeth earlier? Xan would've stopped her if she'd known. Instead, Xera and Spaeth had maneuvered Xan into a position where they could use her and destroy her.

"Damn, I haven't been able to collect all the items I need." He'd been too distracted by a sexy purple demon to gather a part of her. And Spaeth was nearing impossible. It could still be done, but he'd have to sneak around to avoid assassination attempts. He didn't savor asking Xan at the moment. It would be too much like booting her when she was down.

"You can leave at any time, Q." Xan sat up, her clothing rumpled and askew. She didn't bother to straighten it. "You can both go. Go, save the underworld." Sarcasm dripped from her voice.

Stryke didn't have as much compassion as he did. "And you're fine ignoring Xera? Is there no inclination to seek justice or to save future innocents from her hate?"

"Nope."

"What's wrong with you?" Stryke shoved to his feet and stalked toward her.

This could get ugly if Quution didn't step in. "Stryke, enough."

She glared at his brother. "I'm sorry, I should pick up your mission why? I don't recall you ever giving a shit about me or Xera until we interfered with your plans. I don't recall your brother pausing for one moment when I told him how much having access to this realm meant to me. I fail to see why I should waste one more moment in the underworld." She settled back on the sofa, her arms draped over the back, her feet kicked out between Stryke's. "That is, until you suck us back there without a chance to leave."

Stryke gave her a flat look. "You're sinking into a well of self-pity just because your sister did what demons do best?"

Quution repressed his groan. "Stryke, you're not helping."

Stryke didn't budge. "Neither is coddling her during her funk party." His glare hardened. "It's the underworld. None of us had idyllic family lives. All of us have been betrayed by those who should love us. You like this realm so damn much, then save it from the underworld."

From the mutinous look on Xan's face, the tough-love approach wasn't working.

"Get. Out." If she had fangs, they'd be bared.

Quution laid a hand on Stryke's shoulder. "Stryke, wait for me outside."

Stryke's lips were flat. With one last measuring glare at Xan, he nodded and stormed out the door.

Quution sank to his knees in from of Xan. She was still reclined, staring dully at the TV.

"Xan, our realm could really use your help."

She laughed. "Since when."

Since she realized how terrorizing it could be. He sighed. "I can't force you, I can only ask you to help me. I don't think

I can fight your sister and Spaeth and every other demon who'd love to kill me by myself."

"You have Stryke."

Quution winced at the bitterness in her voice. "I don't know how much longer I will have him without your help. If he gets killed, I…don't know what I'll do."

She briefly squeezed her eyes shut and her expression softened.

Perhaps he'd been wrong about how to help her. She needed to nurse her broken heart and deal with the betrayal. Stryke thought she should see how normal the occurrence was for the underworld. But perhaps she had to be shown that there were still supportive, functional relationships in that realm.

"I know it's hard to see," he began, "but there are parents in our realm that love their children and try to protect them. There are siblings who truly have each other's backs, and there are couples who are dedicated to each other."

"Oh yeah? Who?" she challenged.

Quution paused. He racked his brain for examples and came up woefully short. "You know my story. And Stryke's, somewhat. Remember Fyra?"

"The fire demon who used to serve Rancor?"

"She was very close with her mother. And then there's Mantis and Jester."

Xan gave him a sidelong look.

"Hear me out. They *are* dedicated to each other. They have despicable habits and force people into their orgies, but they are loyal to each other."

It was a shitty example, but he didn't get out and socialize in his realm.

"It only makes sense that there are others like us. They need our help." Her sister's abilities were terrifying.

Credits rolled on the show she'd been watching. A quick

announcement about a missing couple filled the screen. Locals, middle-aged. Their family feared something bad had happened to them with the way they'd up and disappeared. Before the couple's image had faded, another episode started almost immediately, a grim narrator accounting the tale of a serial killer who stalked women before stabbing them to death. "A man who thrived on women's fears," the narrator said.

Would Xan see the correlation? This realm wasn't perfect, but she could do good in her own realm.

Xan stood and stretched. Marcus was a good foot taller than his host and twice as wide, packed with solid muscle. Quution wasn't used to being towered over.

Xan dropped her arms, looked him in the eye, and said, "You'd better get going then." She strode to the bathroom, not even slamming the door behind her.

Quution dropped his head. He'd lost her. And if he got the wards back in place, she'd get sucked back into the under-world. And down there, as a shell of herself, she wouldn't last long.

CHAPTER 21

$\mathcal{B}$y the time Xan had finished in the bathroom, Quution was gone. He'd probably driven his host back to her place, got her nice and comfortable, then transported back to the underworld. Such a responsible demon.

The thread of disappointment was stronger than she'd expected. Looking inside her, she started. Marcus wasn't as dormant as he'd appeared, and he didn't like that Brooklyn had left.

Figured. Her host had the hots for Quution's host. It wasn't just attraction that was making Marcus stir. He'd missed a few days of work thanks to her and it was bothering him. Xan checked his phone. Five missed calls and an inbox full of boring insurance questions.

She wasn't ready to let Marcus take control of his own body. Then she'd be stuck with her thoughts. And her regrets.

Taking a note from Quution's book, she got out Marcus's laptop. For no good reason, she searched the history and read over a couple of applications, skimming Brooklyn's address. Huh, she only lived a couple of miles from here.

Xan hit delete on them all and then emptied the trash. Quution would've done so himself, but he probably hadn't planned on leaving so suddenly. If Marcus had mad computer skills, he could retrieve them, but Xan had done what she could.

Hours of reading through emails and listening to voice-mails was finally enough to get her to shower and change clothes.

She was even restless.

Her stomach growled. Too bad there was nothing good in the kitchen. Marcus groused a little at the prospect of diving into the ice cream. And after the sour stomach of the other night, Xan couldn't look at the gallon.

She dug through the cabinets and fridge. No appealing food stood out to her, but she let muscle memory take over until a peanut butter protein shake sat in a glass on the counter.

"Fuck, Marcus. How do you stand yourself?" She pinched her nose to drink it, but as the artificially sweet flavor caressed her tongue, she let go of her nostrils.

Not bad.

She sat back down at the computer but couldn't bust out more than an hour of work. Marcus needed somebody to brighten his boring life. Of course, his last girlfriend had gotten him possessed by a demon, so she couldn't fault his self-imposed isolation. But he shouldn't let his past taint all his future relationships.

Xan froze, her fingers poised over the keyboard. She was reading too much into a simple thought.

The restless energy didn't dissipate. Marcus was an active guy and he'd just lain around for days without being sick.

Fine. She'd go for a run.

Digging through his drawers, she found a spare set of sunglasses. His main pair was in his car, which was still at the gym. Maybe she could run there and grab it. She grabbed his keys and ran out.

The jog to the gym cleared the residual fog from her mind. Marcus was coming around and he'd put up more of a fight for his body soon, but she wasn't ready to relinquish it. She could let him take over, but then she'd give up sunshine, cable TV, and king-sized beds. The only other option was to return to the realm where her deceitful sister was trying to take over.

Nah, she'd hold on as long as she could.

The drive back was uneventful, and when she arrived, she wasn't ready to go back into that apartment. So she took off again.

Inhaling large lungfuls of fresh air, she relaxed into the run. There was no way she could do this in the underworld. Flowering trees on the boulevards released the most delightful fragrances.

Xan sneezed. Then sneezed again.

Was Marcus allergic? Was that why he lived in the gym? Or was she too used to brimstone lacing every scent that she reacted to them as foreign?

Another sneeze and she veered out of the residential areas into a multicomplex community. She passed a street sign and stopped, lurching forward from the sudden lack of momentum.

"For fuck's sake, Marcus."

Brooklyn lived two blocks away.

Xan put her hands on her hips and stretched her chest out. She hadn't realized how much she'd been pushing the pace until she was out of rhythm and sucking oxygen.

Wandering in small circles, she waited until she'd caught her breath. A block ahead, two people walked shoulder to shoulder.

Lurched was more like it.

She spun to head back, but turned again. They were headed for Brooklyn's apartment building in their faded, grungy clothing. Granted, this wasn't the most affluent part of town, but this couple didn't seem like they had a roof over their heads. Their clothing didn't get that sun-bleached without being outside for several days or weeks.

Xan spun around again. The couple could have an apartment and still spend a lot of time outside.

Her feet wouldn't move. She turned back and followed them, keeping her footsteps light.

Marcus's long strides caught up with them in no time.

The woman of the couple turned back to shoot him a glare and a sneer.

Xan cocked her head. It wasn't a normal sneer. It was what she did when she wanted to flash her fangs. Frizzy brown hair hung over the eyes. Xan couldn't tell what color they were other than dark.

How dark? There was a huge difference between rich brown irises and full-on ink-black eyeballs. Xan's shades hid her own telltale eyes.

A niggle in the back of her mind bugged her until she paid attention to it. There was something familiar about this couple.

The woman murmured something to the man before they crossed the street to Brooklyn's apartment. He nodded and faced them. She continued on.

Xan's sickly feeling didn't make her think the woman was going to visit a friend.

The man's unruly hair wasn't enough to cover his eyes and from the way he was grinning, he'd meant for her to see the darkness in his eyes. Behind him, the woman tugged on the heavy glass entry door. It didn't budge. And the woman obviously didn't have keys. What were the odds at least one demon was up to something in the same building as Brooklyn, Quution's host?

Xan studied the man. Recognition tingled through her mind. The middle-aged guy in front of her was demon possessed and not afraid to try to scare her with it. His clothing had been quality at one time. Khakis and a polo shirt that had faded to a greenish camo look.

"Are you following us, bro?" The cultured voice didn't fit the statement.

Marcus was jittering inside her. The answer was on the tip of her—

Aha! This was the couple who'd been missing for months. Pinnacles of society. He'd run a car wash that hosted fundraisers for youth groups and she was a former addict who ran a respected halfway house downtown. The announcement streamed constantly over the TV. One had played earlier today before she'd shut the TV off.

Xan's heart twisted. They'd just lost a kid. That was how the demons had gotten to them.

Why? When there were so many other hosts who played around with the occult, why this couple?

Xan knew the answer without being told. Because they could. Because their grief made the possession more fun.

She slowly removed her shades, letting her eyes answer the demon's question.

He hissed, revealing yellowed teeth that had probably done time in braces. A nice, normal couple ruined by half-breed demons.

Her kind sucked.

"My turn for a question," she said. The exterior door of the apartment building rattled and the woman shrieked. There wasn't time to waste. "Why are you here, and who do you work for?"

Xan's attention peeled off the male. The woman backed

up and took a run at the door. Did the crazy demon think it could break through reinforced glass with a human body?

A thud shook the door and the woman flopped backward. She rolled to her side and popped up. And backed up again.

That demon was going to kill the human.

"No!" Xan lunged forward, but the man in front of her sidestepped into her path. She shoved him off and ran across the street.

In one of the windows, curtains were pulled back and Brooklyn's pert face peeked out. Her brows were drawn when she took in the scene at the door, but when her gaze landed on Marcus, her eyes flew wide.

The man charged and jumped on Xan's back. She grunted and stumbled, dropping her shoulder to flip the guy off. He hit the ground with an *oomph*.

The door rattled again as the woman banged off it. Her body made a sickening thud against the ground, but the woman rolled to her hands and knees to get up again.

"You're not going to break it like that, you idiot." Xan didn't know what else to say to get her to stop. The human's body couldn't take much more.

He glanced up at Brooklyn's window. She had a phone to her ear.

Damn it. She was probably calling the cops. Living in a place like this, she probably didn't take a wait-and-see approach.

The woman was on her feet, swaying, and now the man was as well.

"The cops are coming." Xan couldn't hear sirens yet. "You two need to leave, and if I hear of you coming back, I'll hunt you down."

Xan couldn't get a good sense of who the two demons were.

The woman smiled, blood trickling down her face to stain her chin. "Spaeth wants the host killed."

Spaeth had spies. How had she forgotten? Quution switched hosts so frequently, she hadn't worried, and she'd assumed Spaeth either didn't know or didn't care who her host was. But these two minions had probably found Brooklyn by spying on Marcus's place the last few days. They hadn't gotten close enough for Quution to sense them. So it made sense that they hadn't recognized Marcus if they'd only seen him from a distance and not usually in a hoodie.

The man leered up at the window. Brooklyn slinked back, letting the curtains fall shut. With strength Xan hadn't expected out of the human couple, the man grabbed the woman and threw her into the plate glass door. He crashed after her, using her body weight and his unnatural strength to finally smash through. Glass splintered, parts of the door shattering, the rest cracking into ragged edges.

The couple landed in a tangle on the other side. The poor human woman's legs had been slashed and impaled by shards of glass. The guy pushed off her and took off up the stairs.

Xan crouched and jumped through the opening, sharp edges tearing at her clothing. She paused to check for signs of life in the woman. Unconscious and barely breathing, she bled through her clothing onto the floor. Xan pried an eyelid up. No blackness. Regardless of whether she survived and the demon left her alone, her life was ruined.

Sprinting up the stairs, Xan chased down the human man. He was beating on Brooklyn's door, using the same method as his partner, only this door wasn't as solid as the exterior one.

Bursts of screams inside from a terrified Brooklyn spurred Xan down the hall. She charged to tackle the man, but he ducked out of her way. Xan tripped trying to stop herself and tumbled to the floor, but she jumped up again to face the human. Spinning, the guy aimed a solid kick where the deadbolt would be.

The door splintered open, swinging slow and ominous, and the man stepped inside. "Here kitty, kitty, kitty."

Brooklyn didn't respond. Xan hoped she was tucked into a corner and hidden from sight. Running into the apartment, her heart sank. There were no corners to hide in. The space was too small, too open. A laptop was open on the tiny table by the kitchenette. A futon that was currently functioning as the couch took up most of the living room.

The only other room was the bathroom. That had to be where Brooklyn was hiding. Xan tensed to lunge at the human stalking toward the closed door.

He closed his hand around the knob. "Come out, come out, wherever you are, worthless human."

Xan was about to take him down when he turned the knob and pushed the door open. Why hadn't Brooklyn locked it?

Sirens blared in the distance. Xan was partly relieved, for Brooklyn's sake, but, well, she'd just fucked over Marcus by putting him in the middle of a crime scene.

Xan was readying herself to jump on the man before he laid a finger on Brooklyn when the yellow-daisy-covered shower curtain flew open. A heavy frying pan swung out and clanged against the man's skull. He dropped. Xan wouldn't be surprised if the demon inside had vacated the body before impact.

Brooklyn's hands shook as she gripped the handle and stepped out of the bathtub. Tears streaked her cheeks and a beat of relief passed through her before she met Xan's gaze.

A gasp echoed off the walls of the compact room and she tightened her grip.

Her eyes—Marcus's eyes were black and Brooklyn was experienced enough to know what that meant.

Xan held up her hands, pointing her fingers at herself. "His name is Marcus and he's a good guy. A really good guy, and he was tricked into hosting me. I'm leaving him now."

And with that, she released her hold on him and went back to the underworld.

What would happen to Marcus? Would he get the blame? Would his reputation be destroyed so badly he lost the business he'd worked so hard to build? Brooklyn would be fine. The human couple's life was irrevocably altered at best.

Brimstone surrounding her, Xan opened her eyes in the same spot she'd left in, the same place she'd fought her sister.

She had to find Quution. Because he was right. The human realm was better off without them.

CHAPTER 22

Quution tucked the box containing his items under his arm and scurried down the corridor. The personal wards to his chamber had held, but several demons had tried to break in while he was gone. His home was no longer safe, not for him and not for the materials he needed to carry out his mission. Earlier, he'd stopped at his library and found the same thing, except with singe marks all around the entrance.

As he fled his place, feeling like a coward, he ran through what he still needed in his head.

A piece of Spaeth and Xan. Spaeth was never in one place long enough to grab a part of him, like blood or hair, and he had no scales or horns that molted. And Xan. Quution sighed. He'd spent all that time with Xan and not once had he thought to collect a part of her. She had no hair to pluck a strand of. He'd scored her with his fangs during passion but hadn't been cognizant enough, or willing enough, to say, "Just a moment while I store this drop in a vial."

He'd failed, and now the realm might suffer for it.

There was one place he knew no one would look for him. Maybe one person, but Quution doubted she cared enough at the moment to trek there and destroy his items.

Scrolls were tucked into his pockets and stacks of books were balanced under his other arm. He didn't need free hands to wield his energy, but an attack could derail everything he'd worked and studied for. The way Spaeth and Xera had turned the Circle against him and Xan, he couldn't safely show his face anywhere.

Melody was securely ensconced in the other realm, but Stryke had heard rumors Spaeth's servants were working on spells to summon her back. The same with Xan. Yank the two females to a specified location and execute them.

Quution had to work fast to keep that from happening. He was fairly sure he could resist a summons, and aside from striving to keep Xan and Melody alive and protected, if they were somehow foisted from the Circle, he'd have to regather items for the realm wards from whoever replaced them.

The stench of rotting flesh reached him before he saw the three demons. They had appeared behind him. One must be a tracker, the same demon who'd found his chamber and the library. And they'd managed to sneak up on him. The demons were becoming less afraid of him and his power and learning to work around it.

Quution didn't bother turning around, but he did stop. "Let me ask you one question before we get started." He sensed half-breeds. "Are you working for yourself, or for a full-blooded demon?" Now he faced them.

"Why does it matter?" one male asked, his words garbled like he had a mouth full of pebbles.

"Because your master is not interested in bettering your life, but I am."

"You lie. You're seeking to permanently bond us to our

masters." The demon—who could almost pass in the human realm with a bath and a shave—spat a sizzling glob on the ground. "Then you don't have to waste your energy controlling us."

So that was the ruse Spaeth was going for. Xera might not be as strong as Xan, but she was good. Her power was limited to one use at a time, but all she'd done was plant a seed and allowed current fears and suspicions to flourish. The universal fear in all half-breeds was their greatest weakness as a people. They were weaker and would forever lose what power they had. The fear that kept on giving. And Xera had given them all a common enemy and fostered hope that with Quution's death, their chances for permanent slavery diminished.

He was so screwed.

"I don't waste my energy controlling you." It was useless to argue, but running wouldn't help. It'd only lure them to the safe haven he had in mind.

"You don't need to. You have all the other full-bloods to help you."

Caught by his own lie.

The three advanced together. Quution clung to his items and made one last attempt at reason, knowing deep down it'd fail. "Your mind is being messed with. Your weaknesses tampered with. Spaeth has a purple demon working for him."

The third smiled, revealing a row of sharpened teeth. A set of gills and he'd look like a piranha. "You're the one with a purple girlfriend. You're using her against us. You've enslaved one of the Circle."

The others hissed. As if that wasn't the very thing Spaeth had done. It was a sacrilegious act, to treat one of their leaders as nothing but a half-breed pawn for personal use. Their very worst fear realized.

Quution send out a wire of energy to trip them up. It worked, but it didn't stop them.

The demon with the razor teeth disappeared in a puff of smoke.

Sweet brimstone, a smoke demon. This was bad.

Quution put his back to the wall and cast a dome of pure energy around him. His source was his own power and that of the demons. A ball of smoke bounced off and the demon cried out as he materialized and hit the floor on his bare ass.

The other two attacked the force field, trying to pound through it by sheer force. Their efforts were diminished thanks to being robbed of their own energy by Quution.

But the smoke demon vanished again and a pit formed in Quution's stomach. His bubble wasn't perfect. It had too many openings for one who could turn into smoke. He set the books and the box at his feet, ready to defend himself with claws, horns, and fangs. He wasn't as worried for himself as he was about the items on the floor. If even one of them were destroyed, his entire plan crumbled.

"Oh, boys." Xan's sexy voice carried down the hall.

Quution and the two demons battering his energy stopped and stared at her. She slinked down the hallway, her hips kicking out with each step.

Her own energy had returned, and the guile was back in her eyes.

He smiled and froze as he registered a presence next to him too late.

Sharp claws stabbed his side. He punched out before he turned to look. The demon puffed back into smoke and Quution's arm flung all the way out and hit the wall. Pain burned through his hand, but he dropped to a fighting stance, his focus attuned to the base of his bubble. The smoke demon could exploit any opening.

He wasn't worried about Xan taking care of the other

two. The immediate threat against making everyone safe in the underworld was the smoke demon.

A faint sizzling of energy in front of him tickled his skin. He lashed out with his claws before the smoke demon reformed. He broke skin, and one of his claws jabbed the demon's eye.

A strangled cry scarred his eardrums and the smoke demon staggered back into the electrical field. Quution focused his energy on the areas the demon touched.

He remained fully formed, jerking, as jolts of electricity zapped his body. When his eyelids finally drifted shut, Quution eased up. The demon hit the floor in a lump, unconscious.

Dropping the field, he prepped for another attack, but Xan had the situation dealt with. The other two demons were dragging themselves away, scratched and bleeding.

"Oh, don't forget your friend. Spaeth's hunting for all of you."

The two scrambled to haul their unconscious pal with them. Xan watched them until they disappeared around the corner. Quution couldn't take his eyes off the magnificent female. Less than a day ago, she'd been despondent and watching cable TV reruns. Yet here she was now, back to save his ass.

She met his admiring gaze. "I gave them the impression Spaeth was working with you on all this, and he would find their mates and slaughter them for hurting you." She shrugged. "Not ideal, but it'll wear off and they'll realize I fooled them."

"Spaeth would hunt their mates just for fun," Quution agreed. He wanted to ask why she'd returned, but it didn't seem right as he stood over all the material that could cause her worst fears to come to fruition.

"You're right," she said.

This was Xan, right? And not Xera messing with him? Xan was his greatest weakness, after all. "About?"

She pointed to the pile at his feet. "I think I might've gotten Marcus thrown in jail because I went for a jog past Brooklyn's place and found two demons stalking her. They broke in, and I stopped them, with help from her and a frying pan. Four humans' lives damaged in under five minutes."

He bowed his head. "I'm sorry."

"For what? I've wasted days. It's time to hunt my sister down and stop her." Xan's hard edge was belied by her throat working up and down. "Where are you going?"

"To the cell I was raised in. I don't have everything I need for the realm wards."

She nodded. "Lead the way."

He didn't question his good fortune, picking up his items instead. The rest of the journey only took fifteen more minutes, a mile of passages, and a slide down a narrow tunnel.

He lit a torch to illuminate the area and set his things down. He wasn't going into the cell. He couldn't do it. But the antechamber was enough.

"So what do you need to finish this?"

"A piece of you and Spaeth." He opened the box that contained hair from him and Melody, fur from two other demons. A couple of scales, an egg from Mantis, bits of busted horns and claws from three demons, a vile of acid spit, and two vials of blood. "These are parts of every other Circle member except you two."

"Got an empty vial?" she asked.

He plucked one out of his coat pocket and handed it to her. Her movements were efficient and her face determined as she pricked a finger and let a drop fall into the vial.

Capping it, she handed it back. He set the bottle in the box and slid it into the cell. He wouldn't go inside, but his stuff could.

"Spaeth's going to be tricky," she said. "But he spits when he talks so getting his spit might be the easiest. We can work together. I'm sure Xera's with him."

Quution closed the distance between them. It was too nice to be close to her again, the real her. "Xan, I…"

"Shh. It sucks, but it has to be done. I've seen just a little of the damage they want to do." Sadness filled her eyes. He didn't know if she was mourning the family she'd thought she had, the trouble Marcus and Brooklyn were in, or that she had to fight her sister, but he wanted to make her feel better.

He ran his knuckles along her cheek. She threw her arms around his neck and planted her mouth on his. He staggered back until his back hit the stone slats of the cell.

Her tongue was in his mouth and she lifted her legs and wrapped them around his waist.

If this was how she wanted to feel better, he was on board.

He kissed her like the starving male he was. Hungry for a soft touch—or rough in the right circumstances. He was ravenous for someone of his own. A partner, a lover, a friend. Xan filled all those roles and she'd just fought by his side. And he planned on leaving her.

Gripping her ass cheeks and careful of his claws, he turned and tread forward until her back touched the slats. He barely noticed that she was kissing him around his fake fangs. All he cared about was not hurting her.

As if she sensed that he couldn't untie his pants without shanking her or impaling his dick with his stupid claws, she wormed a hand between them.

Her hand went straight for his cock. His pelvis jacked forward like it had a mind of its own and one goal—to get closer to her. She let go only to yank the tie at his waist. His pants hit the floor and she circled his erection with her hot hand.

She released his mouth, her other arm anchored around his neck, and rocked up until the head of his shaft rubbed along her slit.

All he could do was groan.

"It's been too long," she whispered.

He agreed. It'd only been a few days since he'd been with her, but he could spend the rest of his days loving her over and over again. Her juices coated him, but he didn't push her. She would set the pace.

And she chose excruciatingly slow.

She shifted until he was pressing inside of her, but she didn't drop down until he was buried to the hilt. She took him one inch at a time and let him watch the desire, the yearning, the craving.

They were both seeking solace in the other. Proof that what they had could transcend spells and wards and realms. Reassurance that this wouldn't be their last time.

He trembled as he held himself still. Finally, he was buried completely inside her, connected.

"Xan—"

She pressed a finger to his lips that smelled of ripe sex, causing his fangs to throb. He sucked her finger into his mouth and twirled his tongue around the tip.

Her pupils flared, making her eyes fathomless. He could get lost in them forever. But his time here was limited. His plans were about more than what he wanted.

Xan arched her back as much as she could, pinned between him and the wall. He thrust up as she crashed back down. Over and over, they slammed into each other, seeking release, clinging to the other.

He slid in and out, her walls gripping him, her core blazing hot. His energy trickled out, crackling over her skin like tiny fireworks. Her lips parted and her legs tightened.

"Qu—" A moan rolled out and her eyes squeezed shut. She shattered in his arms and it was glorious, the most beautiful thing he'd ever seen.

His climax claimed him instantly. He couldn't hold her shuddering in his arms from pleasure he'd given her and not get pushed past his peak.

He buried his head in the crook of her neck. Releasing inside of her was an experience he'd cherish forever. Every second he got to spend with her was a treasure, the reading lessons, the first hallucination, even the times when she needled him for information.

He'd take all of those memories to the other side with him.

~

XAN TRIED to disguise the trembling in her hand as she sorted through scrolls. Quution was bent over them, pointing out various details to Stryke. Her male was as calm and practical as he always was. Meanwhile, she fought down a constant titter over their mad coupling. Her body wanted to melt into a puddle while her mind wanted to break down and cry over the depth of their connection.

It couldn't be their last time. It just couldn't. She'd reconciled herself to him leaving when she'd had the chance to be reunited with her family. But now she would be alone once this was over.

Melody had arrived in the underworld a few minutes ago, like an obnoxious ray of sunshine. Her bright hair reflected the torchlight, and the flowery vines she'd covered herself in bloomed with pale pink petals. It was like death by happiness. But Xan was warming up to her. She'd tried not to. Melody would be in her own realm when Quution finished the job. It was no use getting friendly with the female when she'd be just another person to mourn the loss of soon.

Xan's future was dark. But she was willing to make the sacrifice. She could spend her days alone, hiding in the honeycomb of the underworld.

The other female was casting her own curious looks Xan's way. The few times Xan had interacted with her previously, she'd purposely twanged Melody's insecurities. If the female held a grudge, Xan would understand, but they were weaknesses that'd had to be addressed at the time. Melody was already nursing a major inferiority complex because she'd been born human and was ruling an underworld full of demons.

That was going to change, though. Melody would be out of a job soon—if they could track down Spaeth, bottle some spit, and get out alive. And of course, find Xera.

"If anything happens to me," Quution was telling Stryke, "it's all here."

A muscle flexed in Stryke's jaw. "Nothing's going to happen to you." He beckoned Xan and Melody over. Choosing a bare spot outside of the cell, he squatted and scratched a sharp nail in the dirt. "Here's where the Circle meets. I've traced Spaeth's energy signature four corridors down."

"Mm." He'd moved then. His new digs were two corridors over from where Xan had met with him. Coward. "I bet he controls that whole section."

Quution leaned over Stryke and gestured to the far corner of his drawing. "Xan's correct. That was where we found Xera."

Xan would find her sister again. Xera was blazing through the Circle, crazing half-breeds and making them attack each other.

Stryke tapped a finger on the opposite side of Spaeth's area. "Melody and I come in from the back. You and Xan from the front. And we surround him."

"Can't he just poof away?" Melody asked.

"Spaeth appears and disappears, but he can't teleport," Xan explained. "He just goes incorporeal, and when he does, his radiation goes as well." Until he took form again and burned everyone around him.

Creaks of vines and plants came from Melody. She was using her plant power to cover herself in a suit of barky armor.

Fuck, that was cool.

Melody's horns gleamed. A drop of toxin hung off each one. Her sunny packaging hid a poisonous, deadly demon.

Yeah, they could've been good friends.

"Ready?" Stryke asked.

"Once Spaeth is defeated, you two get out of the realm. You can't risk getting caught down here." Quution left "or I'd never forgive myself" unsaid, but Xan heard the vulnerability in his voice and hated it. Xera could latch on to his fears of getting his friend and his brother trapped in the underworld.

Stryke left with Melody. Their trip would take them longer, but they weren't being hunted at the moment and would run into less trouble than she and Quution would.

Quution shuffled his gaudy boots. "We should leave, too, as we'll have to duck and cover to avoid conflict."

Xan eyed him. False fangs and claws were in place. Ratty clothes. Uneven shoes.

"Get naked," she ordered.

"Uh…We don't have time to…"

"No." She was done with deception. Quution was going to

lock the entire underworld in the realm, and every demon down here needed to know exactly who'd done it. She twirled her finger at him. "You need to lose the disguise. A half-breed is putting the realm on lockdown. Let our kind own that shit. Not to mention, it'll help us get through the corridors. It's going to take a moment for others to recognize you."

Although she didn't know why. With horns the color of sunset and lilac eyes, he was clearly Quution whether he was outfitted full-blood style or delightfully bare.

He pondered her words for a few moments. She thought he might reject her idea, but then he tossed his coat off. Next came his baggy undershirt, then the pants she'd dropped not long before. He stepped out of his boots and shoved them aside with his foot. She winced as he yanked the fangs out, then pried each claw off.

Rolling his neck and flexing his hands, he groaned. "I'm actually a little nervous."

Her lips twitched. No demon would be caught dead admitting to a case of the nerves, but Quution wasn't an average demon. She eyed his full length. Definitely above average.

"The real demon Q is about to take this place down." He smiled and she liked seeing his lips unencumbered by his fangs. But the grin faded. "Xan, when we…" His eyes turned tortured, his look haunted.

She stepped close and draped her hands on his chiseled chest. "I didn't come back here for you to stall when we need you the most. I can't afford to think about might-have-beens and lost dreams." Xera would target them soon enough. "If things were different, you and I would hole up in a chamber and forget the world. I'd make it look like that cabin and we could stare out at a pretend sunset every night. But they're not different and this needs to be done."

He didn't touch her and she didn't get any closer to him than she already was. One last regretful look and he lifted the shoebox and secured it in the crook of his elbow. They would launch the wards as soon as a piece of Spaeth was in the shoebox.

"Very well," he said, his expression resolute. "I am ready."

At least one of them was.

CHAPTER 23

Quution struggled not to grab Xan and duck into the next empty chamber. She could create the shared hallucination again and he could pretend to cook for her. He'd even eat candy beetles to keep the ruse going.

Only it wouldn't work. They'd eventually be found, hunted and killed.

He couldn't quit wondering what would happen to her once the wards were in place. The majority of the demons in the realm didn't know she was helping him, and once Xera was dealt with, Xan could take care of those who aimed the blame her way.

All those worries were assuming that they'd succeed. Xera was a fearsome opponent. She didn't have a single soft spot in her heart and that gave her a dangerous edge.

But Spaeth was a full-blooded demon. Ruthless, powerful, and deadly. He wasn't playing around. He wanted Quution gone, and he'd even shown two traits rare in his kind: cunning and patience. He and Xera wouldn't be taken off guard. They'd be expecting trouble.

He and Xan kept marching. The few demons they crossed

paths with all reacted the same. Their gaze lit on Xan, they snarled, then they prepped to attack Quution. Only then did they do a double take, their eyes widening when energy snapped over Quution and they realized who he really was. Then they tripped over themselves running to tell everyone that Quution was a half-breed like them.

Walking naked through the underworld had turned out to be his best defense. His real form provided the truth needed to disrupt Xera's influence over them.

A wave of dread nearly swept him under. He sucked in a breath and tensed.

Xan laid a warm hand on his arm. "It's begun."

Xera.

He and Xan held hands like a junior-high couple. The connection was strong enough to fend off the worst of Xera's attacks. The demon could only alternate between him and Xan; she couldn't maintain her power with both.

In his mind, the image of Stryke crumpling to the ground, covered in bubbling sores from Spaeth's radiation, stopped him in his tracks. "No." He doubled over, his hands on his knees. Xan was right next to him, but Stryke wasn't. What if he and Xan didn't get there in time? What if both Stryke and Melody succumbed to Spaeth? What if—

"Quution?" Xan rubbed his back. "Whatever you're thinking, it's a lie."

"Stryke... He's... He..." Quution squeezed his eyes shut. How could it be a lie? It was so clear. He could even smell skin burning.

"Was Melody in the vision? Because Xera doesn't know Melody's with him and she's only targeting your fears for your brother."

No, Melody wasn't in the vision. He straightened. Xera didn't know him well enough to target all those he cared about.

Xan's eyes widened and she gripped his arm with both hands.

"What are you seeing?" Quution asked.

"You. Same old." She gritted her teeth and dragged him forward.

While they couldn't delay, he suspected Xan wasn't telling him everything. "It'll lose its power if you talk to me," he urged.

She lifted her chin, her eyes full of resolve. "You left me behind. But I've dealt with it. She's sensing the rawness of my emotion, but not that I've come to terms with what you need to do."

His chest ached like Xera had flayed him open and clawed out his heart. He was leaving Xan. One way or the other. He could die saving her, and that might mean they lost the battle against Spaeth. But if they won, he'd be sealing himself on the other side.

This sucked.

Xan's claws pinched his skin. Her sister's attack was getting worse, but since it wasn't stopping Xan, he'd guess it was Xera who was growing more erratic.

"Two more lefts and we'll be back at his chamber," Quution said. Facts. Facts fight the fears.

She nodded. "He won't be there. He's a coward and he'll launch a—"

A dart skimmed past her face to imbed in the wall. She jumped back and Quution slid in front of her. He didn't look to see who it was before he whipped out a coil of energy that followed the path of the dart.

A yelp and a snarl gave him a grim smile. He'd hit his target. Since that dart belonged to a being who most certainly wanted to hurt them, he flung out shot after shot of energy. The snarls turned to cries, then to screams.

Xan sidled around him, skimming the edges of the

corridor to keep from getting hit, and turned the corner. Her nose wrinkled.

"That answers the question of whether venom is flammable or not." Her eyes flew wide and she flung her hand out. "Stop! It's one of the Circle full-bloods."

He withdrew the final bolt of energy he'd intended to throw and jogged to her side. A heap of charred full-breed was on the ground. Quution had almost ruined everything.

"Is he dead?" Xan slipped closer.

He tested the waves coming off the demon. "No, but close. He's healing as we speak." That had been close. But if he could do the same thing to Spaeth without killing him, they'd be home-free. "But he should stay down long enough for us to get done what we need to get done."

He sensed the readings in their surroundings and steered Xan around the other way.

"The full-breed was a decoy, but Spaeth must have more working with him." He tensed as new vibrations trickled over him. "Including the two half-breeds approaching."

Quution handed his box to Xan and balled up energy in his hand, muting the light coming off it to keep them concealed.

A male's voice sounded from around the corner. "I can't wait until that stupid host heals. I want to throw her against the door again. The sound was delightful."

Xan's lip curled, her fangs shiny in the torchlight. "He's the one who went after Brooklyn."

Quution split his orb into two, one for each hand. When the couple turned the corner, he aimed and launched each one.

The female dodged hers, swiveling to the side. A strangled cry ripped out of the male as the bolt cleaved his chest. Quution fired a second shot, hitting the male's neck and finishing him off. The stench of burnt skin filled the air.

It would be the smell of the night.

Snarls mingled with death throes. The female charged them. She bobbed and wove, effectively keeping him from targeting her like he had her partner.

Xan didn't stand around and wait. She sprinted, bounded off the wall, and twisted in midair to catch the female around the neck. Her momentum carried the female with her, but not fast enough for her body to keep up with the rotation. A crack rent the air.

Xan released her opponent and landed on her feet. "Mind doing the honors? I don't have a blade and I don't think a simple broken neck will stop this one."

A trickle down Xan's side caught his attention. "You're bleeding. Wait—are you really bleeding?" He had to make sure he wasn't hallucinating.

She touched her side. "Yes. The bitch's horn cut me."

Alarm punched him in the gut, and he knelt by the female. "Do her horns have toxins?"

"Probably. But we gotta keep going."

He glanced up into her dark eyes. What if she'd been poisoned? Some venom was medicinal, some hallucinogenic, others, like Melody's, affected the body in a specific way. But some were just lethal. What if the substance in Xan was deadly?

"Quution."

She was fine. For now. But she couldn't hide the worry in her eyes from him.

"I'm not irrationally scared at the moment. You?" Xan kept wanting to look over her shoulder. They had to be close to Spaeth's lair. Black markings on the walls looked just like the kind he left behind whenever he loosed his radiation on some poor bastard.

She was about to be the poor bastard.

"No. I'm strangely centered," Quution answered. "Perhaps Xera is busy with Stryke and Melody."

She heard the uneasiness in his voice. He'd never forgive himself if tragedy struck his brother or the female. And Xan was experiencing her own odd anxiety over it. She wasn't besties with either one, but they were decent halflings and she'd hate to see them gone.

Her stomach roiled and it wasn't due to her nerves. A heaviness had settled into her muscles and she fought the urge to yawn. She didn't know the demon she'd taken down, but the female had managed to inject her with something.

Dammit. Quution didn't need a hindrance, and if she crawled into a corner to take a nap, she'd get them both killed.

"Xan." Quution's hand was on her arm as he peered at her. She knew that look. He was reading her energy.

"I think her poison was a sedative." How wickedly convenient for a demon. Put their prey to sleep, then kill, accost, or eat. "I didn't get a huge dose." She tried for a light note. "But I might need a snooze after this is all said and done."

He peered even closer until she could drown in the pools of his light eyes. His hand tightened on her. "Fact. Damn, I was hoping it was your sister messing with me."

"Not this time," she said sadly.

A female's cry made them both spin their heads toward one direction.

"Melody."

She and Quution took off at a sprint. Thankfully, he hadn't let her go, and she used his hold on her to propel her forward. Her feet were like stone bricks and she lost the battle to yawn.

Another shriek of outrage greeted them as they rounded the corner toward Spaeth's lair. Only he wasn't in his chamber. He was down the hall in the opening to an uninhabited cavern.

Melody's vines were smoking as Spaeth appeared and disappeared around her. Stryke was grappling with Xera. Her sister moved too fast to get tangled in Stryke's energy webs or hit by an orb, and she landed a punch, then a claw on the male.

"Melody, leave the realm!" Quution shouted.

The female would be nuked alive if she lingered much longer. Her movements were erratic and her expression pinched. The burns were getting through her viney armor.

"Melody, trust us," Stryke said between clenched teeth. "Go."

Xan's breath hitched, but that might just be the start of another yawn. Melody's eyes finally filled with resolve. She'd realized she was a liability. Spaeth didn't need Xera to make them lose their shit over the girl's death.

Melody vanished, striking out one last time with a barbed twine before she left. It nailed Spaeth in the eye. He hollered, momentarily staying in one spot longer than Xan had ever seen. He wasn't as tall as the brothers, but he was wider and his skin undulated with heat.

Quution didn't hesitate. He flung a blazing orb. The ball hit Spaeth in the shoulder, and he staggered to the side. But it was nothing more than a distraction. The demon absorbed the hit into itself. Energy unto energy.

Xan pressed her back against the wall across from Spaeth and concentrated. Fatigue was claiming her too fast to physically attack Spaeth, but her powers were still effective.

Until he noticed what she was doing and disappeared.

The four of them paused, but only for a heartbeat. Quution was prepared. He tossed up an energy field to block his part of the corridor. Stryke did the same with his. The five of them were trapped together.

Xera stopped her assault on Stryke to look around, like she was seeking guidance about what to do next. She glanced at Xan, a hateful expression rippling over her face.

Quution was leaving her. He was gone. She was alone again. No one loved her.

The rapid bombardment of negative thoughts clashed in Xan's skull. She hissed and pressed her palms against her eyes.

"It's not real," Quution said.

Spaeth appeared in the doorway, the flash of his heat blasting Xan across the face. He grabbed Xera by the neck and yanked her to him.

Xera shrieked. Her color dulled to an ashen purple, her fingers digging into his and releasing against the agony.

Spaeth pierced her with his retina-searing gaze. "Tell him to lower the fields."

"No," Xan croaked. She threw an *is this real?* look at Quution. At his slow nod, she almost squeezed her eyes shut.

Xera's mouth gaped, but only strangled gurgles came out, her eyes pleading. No matter what her sister had done, Xan couldn't watch her die without doing something.

She pushed off the wall, managing not to sway.

"Don't come closer." The muscles flexed in Spaeth's arm as he tightened his grip and lifted until Xera's toes swept the floor. "Tell. Him."

No noise was coming from Xera. Her eyes were rolled back in her head.

Xan had to make a decision. And it was a brutal one.

Spaeth was going to kill Xera no matter what Quution did. Her sister was of no use to him as he fled like the coward he was.

Spaeth must've read the resolve in her eyes. He stepped

back farther and blazed like a mini nova. Xan threw her arm over her eyes and dove for Spaeth, claws outstretched. She reached beyond her sister and scored Spaeth's side at the same time the bones in Xera's neck were ground to bits, her body folding to the ground. Spaeth didn't bother to toss the lifeless head, just let it fall as he vanished. An enraged bellow followed on the air currents he left behind.

Quution dropped the field. Stryke followed suit, both confident that Xan had gotten what they needed.

Xan hit the ground. She rolled up to her knees but immediately fell on her side. Her energy was gone. She was so tired. Her skin was tight, like she'd lain in full summer sun for days. Her fingers throbbed and blisters formed before her eyes. She cradled her hand like it was fragile crystal. And her sister was gone.

Peeling her eyes open, she searched for Quution. He and Stryke were squatting around her.

"Spaeth's gone," Quution said. "And Xera is…"

"She was already gone to me. Hurry," Xan murmured, her eyelids falling shut. She summoned enough from her reserves to hold her hand out to him. *Please let there be blood or skin under my claw.*

Her breathing slowed. Quution would ward the underworld and be in a different realm when she woke, and she didn't have the energy to say goodbye. But there would be plenty of time to mourn him.

If Spaeth didn't find her first and kill her before she woke.

CHAPTER 24

*X*an's hand went limp in his grip. She was asleep. His arms itched to sweep her up and cradle her until she came to.

Stryke grabbed the shoebox from him and started withdrawing supplies. "Quution. You need to do this."

While Quution could do nothing more than sweep his gaze over the slumbering form of the demon who meant so much to him, Stryke lifted Xan's hand from him. He scraped under the nails, collecting debris like he was a forensic tech.

"We need to get her somewhere safe. Once I leave the realm…" Quution's throat thickened, and he couldn't finish his sentence.

He wasn't ready.

Stryke's mouth tightened. His gaze went from the shoebox to Xan. "You do your thing. I'll secure this room. She'll be safe until she wakes up. You said she can get through our security."

But Spaeth might be waiting for her. Or the rest of the underworld, heavy with a grudge and demanding her death.

"Quution." Stryke sprinted to the door. He peeked out

227

and jerked back, tossing a rippling curtain of energy over the door. "It's not Spaeth, but his servants are coming."

Right. Spaeth would have more than the two servants they'd downed in the corridors.

He gave Xan one last lingering look. Stryke's defenses would hold, but for how long?

"Quution!" Stryke barked. But his eyes were soft with sympathy. "Either you ward this realm, or we fight our way out of here."

Shouts echoed from down the passageways. A horde was coming for them.

He risked both Stryke and Xan with his delay. Quickly laying out all thirteen pieces from the Circle members in a 13-sided star pattern, with his own strand of hair at the top, he started the incantation. Weaving his fingers over the items, he layered spell over spell, binding the realm's energy to itself and using his own for the glue.

Stryke needed to leave, but Quution couldn't bring himself to tell his brother to go. Because Quution would be next and then Xan would be alone. For now, she had both of them defending her.

Chanting, he worked through the spells. So many spells. Stryke blocked the entrance, randomly firing energy balls to keep the demons from seeing what Quution was up to.

The walls of the chamber shook as demons sought to get to them any other way possible.

Quution quieted. Each item disappeared, functioning as approval, as if each member of the Circle were here helping to seal the wards in place. Just one tiny opening remained, and it would be sealed as he and Stryke left, tying the wards shut like a giant, ethereal drawstring bag. Quution only had to bind his energy to the planes of the human realm. All the words were there, he just had to say them. Crouching by Xan, he grasped her hand.

"I can't leave her, Stryke." She'd be vulnerable. She could be killed before she even awoke. But worse, she would be trapped away from him forever.

Stryke spun from the door and pushed a hand through his hair and over his horns. "I'm sorry, but there's no one else who can monitor the wards for eternity. You're the only one strong enough."

"You."

Stryke shook his head. "No. You're more closely tied to this realm, you understand its energy better." He stared at him. "You're stronger."

"Perhaps not. Perhaps…" Quution skimmed a finger down Xan's face. "Perhaps I just wanted an excuse to get myself permanently out of this realm. You have the power. You're from here and you're older than me. You can do it."

Stryke swallowed. "And you?"

"I'll be here. With her."

Stryke's jaw clenched hard. "She's the one."

"Yes." Quution rose slowly. This was goodbye. He wasn't prepared, hadn't expected to have anyone to say goodbye to. But between his brother in the human realm and Xan down here, the choice was clear. Stryke had his mate. Quution had Xan.

Quution swallowed hard and stuck out his hand. "It's been an honor to know you. Be well, Brother."

Stryke grabbed his hand and pulled him in for a hug. Brother to brother.

"Take care of yourself," Stryke said gruffly.

"I shall miss you."

Releasing him, Stryke stepped away. Orbs of energy were balanced in each hand. "I'm leaving this realm in a blaze. Seal the wards and get the fuck out of this chamber."

His brother crossed the curtain of energy and sent blooms of searing energy down each side of the corridor.

Shouts of rage and pain filled the hall just before Stryke disappeared.

Quution concentrated on Stryke's energy signature. When it had left the realm, he uttered the final words.

Demons flooded the entrance, but Stryke's force field held.

Quution gathered a warm and sleepy Xan in his arms. She murmured unintelligible words and curled into him.

His body vibrated with the loose energy he'd reserved for binding himself to the human realm. His determined gaze landed on the exit and he faced it squarely, his precious bundle secured in his arms.

He had no chambers to go to and hers were no longer safe. He'd scour the underworld for a place for them. As long as they were together, it didn't matter where.

CHAPTER 25

*Q*uution stared out the fake window where the pretend lake glittered in the distance. "They've attacked the wards again."

"When did demons get such long memories? They should've moved on and formed new resentments by now," Xan muttered. "I can't believe they're still after you when there's an all-out war between full-bloods and half-breeds."

Between the both of them, they'd seeded the information about the infant sacrifices far and wide until the half-breeds had realized they'd never be able to coexist with full-breeds. Instead, they'd declared their right to rule the realm. And they were winning. Another reason he was glad he'd stayed. Demons were a bad bunch, but perhaps with more opportunity to be good…

Unfortunately, both parties hated him for sealing them down here. Full-bloods because he'd cut them off from their power base—controlling access to human hosts—and of course, for ruining their plans for worlds domination. And half-breeds…well, for essentially the same reasons. It didn't matter if halflings agreed that possession was wrong; it just was, and humans had to deal with it.

So as they fought themselves, they also hunted him and Xan.

She was distant. She'd been aloof for the last couple of days. He tried not to let it bother him, but life had been far less than idyllic during the month they'd spent in their new home.

He never thought he'd spend his final years in the same place he'd clawed his way out of and sworn never to return to. But no one had found him when he was growing up and it had seemed like the best place to set up their fortress.

The difference was, when he was a kid, no one had been looking for him. After word spread about what Quution had done—with Xan's assistance—they'd both become the underworld's most wanted. Apparently sacrificing babies was less atrocious than shutting off access to the human realm.

He had no idea how long they could stay here. Xan's shared hallucination was waning. Already, the illusion of the countryside looked more like a watercolor painting. She needed her power to lead the demon hunters astray and he was happier to be with her than to have a cabin by the lake. It was no longer his weakness to want to live in the human realm, and not just because it was impossible. Spending day and night with nothing to do but Xan was a perfect day, wherever they spent it, marred only by the fear for their safety.

Giving up at the window, he went to the rock situated next to hers, where they dined on candy beetles together. The bugs were growing on him, though he'd probably grow tired of them after an eternity. If they made it that long.

"We need to plan for our future," he said. "I think we may have to move periodically and secure our fortress each time."

She didn't respond, her gaze stuck on the far wall, and it wasn't even the wall with the fake window.

"Xan?"

Her eyes narrowed and she cocked her head, but he didn't think she was listening to him. She was deep in concentration.

The illusion of a tiny cabin disappeared. Dirt walls surrounded him once again.

"Have they launched an attack?" He sensed her funneling all of her energy into her powers.

Her lips spread in a huge grin and her eyes danced. "Eureka!"

"Did you send them running?" He could go for a blissful night of sleep. They had sex together, but they didn't sleep together. One of them always had to be on watch.

"Nope." Her smile was in place and she grabbed his hand. "Is there anything you want to keep in this place?"

He glanced around. All his possessions looked pathetic and useless. It wasn't like they could move them to their next home. Any relocation would be furtive and done in darkness. He and Xan hadn't gathered anything so much as a pebble. It helped aid in the illusion that hordes weren't trying to kill them. "All I need is you."

"Good. Now think of Brooklyn and let's go."

"What—"

As soon as Brooklyn's face popped into his mind, he sensed her energy and he was gone.

His eyes popped open. He was staring at a grinning Marcus. The male's eyes were pure black.

He sat up. Blankets fell from his chest. He glanced down. "Sweet brimstone!" Yanking the covers up, he covered his bare breasts—*Brooklyn's* bare breasts.

Taking in his surroundings, he frowned. Marcus's

bedroom. He was in Marcus's bed. *Brooklyn* was in Marcus's bed.

Xan put her heavily muscled arms behind her head. "I knew I could do it," she said arrogantly.

"What, exactly, did you do?"

"Got through the weakness in the wards."

He stiffened. "The wards have weak points?" He'd studied those spells for years, overlapped them, twisting them into each other.

"Yeah." She thumped her chest with a finger. "Me."

All the times she'd broken into his place ran through his mind. And how she'd gotten into the library and the cell where he'd been raised. She always found her way through his powers. It was like they recognized what she meant to him and allowed her through.

"But *I* couldn't even get through."

"Because you can't sense the vulnerable points." She crossed her feet, smug smile still in place.

He glanced around. They were out of the underworld. Back in their hosts.

But this didn't feet right. He should be jubilant, but he couldn't be. How could he steal one couple's life to live his own? He wouldn't be any better than the demons he'd imprisoned.

One question pushed past his doubts. "What are Marcus and Brooklyn doing together?"

"He was always attracted to her. And a lonely fucker. I bet they're good together."

Quution searched for the answers in Brooklyn's psyche. "She's working for him and he's been able to expand. She's head over heels in love."

"He's healthier and happier and totally in love. *We* did that." Xan chuckled, sounding all kinds of proud of herself.

Quution couldn't join in her elation. "Xan, we can't do this."

She lifted a dark brow. "You know what we can do? Use your mad energy skills to bind yourself to this realm, then bind me to you. I just needed to borrow these guys for a while to see if I could get us back here."

He sputtered, then coughed, then stared at her. All words vacated him and he had only one thought. "You're a damn genius."

"Mm."

"*A*re you sure we have enough food?" Xan said. She scratched the paper with her pen, scowling as the ink slowly ran out, leaving nothing but gouges in the sheet. Tossing the pen, she reached for a new one.

Their friends were going to arrive soon, starting with Demetrius and his mate, Calli. Xan would've thought their friends would have nothing going on, but planning this night had been its own organizational hell. The vampire team might have no demons to fight for a good long while, but their government had its own law enforcement system. Instead of retirement, the vampires had joined in the effort to police Freemont and clean up the vampires who had been conducting clandestine business with the underworld before going into other nefarious activities. As Demetrius liked to say, vampires were always up to something.

None of them could see into the future, and Quution wasn't used to doing nothing. Preparations were being made in the event the realm wards ever fell. She was aiding in those efforts.

First, they had to record what Quution had done to seal

the wards, all his research, in case something ever happened to him. So Quution would recreate the scrolls he'd left behind in the underworld in a weave of energy, like a snapshot from his brain, and she'd write like a maniac. All those hours spent learning to read and write had turned into more than a con to get close to Quution.

Demetrius and Calli were arriving first so Calli could look at what they had transcribed. Quution's condition for such access was that the vampires become the protectors of all demonic scrolls, tomes, and etchings of any sort.

Quution turned toward her and away from the window he'd been staring out. Their real-life cabin was deep in the forest. They had no candy beetles, but Quution donned his hat and sunglasses and made monthly trips to the nearest town for supplies. She'd learned to bake to assuage her sweet tooth. They hunted their meat and grew and cooked the rest.

She knew what he saw when he gazed out the window. A glimpse of the cold blue lake they skinny-dipped in, pine trees, and a midnight sky. She'd caught herself staring out that window several times in the few months they'd been living out here. An illusion come to life.

Stryke and Zoey had helped them buy the land, and Xan got to use her powers occasionally to scare any stray humans away.

"We're going to need a bonfire to cook all the food we have." He stepped away from the window. "Ah. They are arriving."

Xan jumped up. Calli was becoming a good friend, and it helped that she was fascinated by all things demon, including Xan herself.

Quution opened the door a few seconds before Demetrius appeared. The vampire's arm was lovingly wrapped around the tall blonde.

In Calli's hand was a tray of cookies and brownies. "From Betty."

Xan groaned. Demetrius's elderly assistant had been delighted to find another sweet tooth to cater to. "Where has that female been my whole life?"

After the four of them had pored over scrolls for an hour, tossing ideas back and forth, Quution popped his head up.

She grinned and grabbed his hand to run outside. They were both as giddy as humans with their first home.

Rourke appeared with Grace, uttering their thanks for a date night without kids. Fyra and Bishop were next. Quution had shamelessly waited for Fyra. He'd been serious about a bonfire and she was their flame.

Creed appeared, and Melody shrieked and threw herself at Xan. "This place is gorgeous! Did you know there's land for sale adjacent to your property?" She jerked her head toward Creed, her sunny curls bouncing. "He bought it for me. We're neighbors!" Melody took hold of Xan's shoulders and squealed.

Ophelia and Bastian arrived next. Xan was getting to know the deadly female. When they'd first met, Ophelia had eyed her up and down and asked if she needed a sparring partner. Only Ophelia had to flash out here to do it. Xan would have to drive, and a purple demon gathered too much attention behind the wheel. She saved her outings for Halloween.

When Stryke and Zoey arrived, Xan had to stop and look around. The guys ringed the fire Fyra had zapped into existence. The females grouped together, talking excitedly like it'd been years since they'd all been able to chat without interruption. Desserts lined the picnic table Quution had acquired during one of his trips into town. Piles of meat were waiting to be grilled, and laughter rippled over the trees. Moments like these, Xan wondered if one of her kind had cast an epic illusion over her.

And every time Xan was plagued by uncertainty that this was real, Quution was suddenly next to her, his arm around her shoulders, stating facts.

"This is your family, Xan. You have six brothers and six sisters. And me. We're all real."

She clasped her hand over his and planted a kiss on the full lips she finally had unfettered access to. Yes, real. A world not filled with fear, but with joy, and she didn't have to be a full empath to create her own, both within herself and with Quution.

And she did. Every night.

————————

THERE'S a new paranormal series on the horizon. For new release updates, chapter sneak peeks, and exclusive quarterly short stories, sign up for Marie's newsletter and receive download links for the book that started it all, *Fever Claim*, and three short stories of characters from the series.

THANK YOU FOR READING. I'd love to know what you thought. Please consider leaving a review at the retailer the book was purchased from.

~Marie

ABOUT THE AUTHOR

Marie Johnston lives in the upper-Midwest with her husband, four kids, and an old cat. Deciding to trade in her lab coat for a laptop, she's writing down all the tales she's been making up in her head for years. An avid reader of paranormal romance, these are the stories hanging out and waiting to be told between the demands of work, home, and the endless chauffeuring that comes with children.

mariejohnstonwriter.com
Facebook
Twitter @mjohnstonwriter

ACKNOWLEDGMENTS

Thank you to my fearless editor and my first readers for making this the most polished product it can be.

Printed in Poland
by Amazon Fulfillment
Poland Sp. z o.o., Wrocław

64222828R00148